Through the eyes of a young
life of the great hunters of t
style and the words exchange ... vivacity or a graphic novel. . . .
We travel to the heart of an imaginary country, but . . . they are places of
adventure which are the most exceptional habitats and decorated caves
that archaeological science has revealed to the world in the last century
and a half. . . . This saga is therefore also a breathtakingly realistic story
that compels admiration. This story goes far beyond Brian Hayden's
scientific writings; it anchors them in the passion of our society for the
sciences of ancient times.

— Jean-Michel Geneste
Former Chief of Scientific Studies for Chauvet Cave
Former Chief Curator of Lascaux Cave for over twenty years
Former Director of the National Centre of Prehistory
Honorary General Curator of French heritage

Other novelists have tried to capture this time and place, often almost as
sci-fi thrillers, but Hayden's story is different. It rings true in details of
everyday life and of extraordinary moments of the boy's first communal
hunt, his exploration of a forbidden cave and his initiation into the group's
secret society. Hayden demonstrates a novelist's ability to capture
human experiences of friendship, rivalry, love and survival in this vivid
coming of age story. . . . Hayden also provides a comprehensive scientific
knowledge of their lives and achievements . . . to combine them all so
successfully is remarkable. I highly recommend this novel to the young
reader certainly, but really to anyone interested in historical fiction.

— Timothy Earle
Professor Emeritus at Northwestern University, author of *The Evolution of
Human Societies* and numerous works on inequality and social complexity

Behind the fiction, Hayden convincingly reconstitutes the daily life of
these ancient people: the collective hunts, the initiation rites, the art of the
caves and the importance of traditions. . . . A book intended for children
but which describes these prehistoric times in a way much closer to the
reality than occurs in many specialized publications. This book shows
Hayden is not only one of the most renowned ethno-archaeologists, but
also a fine connoisseur of human psychology.

— Emmanuel Guy, Ph.D.
Author of *Préhistoire du Sentiment Artistique*
and *Ce Que l'Art Préhistorique Dit de Nos Origines*
Université Paris I Panthéon-Sorbonne

An engaging tale of survival, rivalry, mysticism and love in the last Ice Age.

— Paul Bahn
Author of *Images of the Ice Age*

Very few people in the world have the knowledge and skill to transport you twenty thousand years into the past. Hayden will embed you in the Bear Clan, and you will see the hunts, the feasts, the initiations, the ceremonies, the loves and griefs of a world that has long disappeared.

— Gabriel Dinim
Weaver, photographer

At first I was skeptical, but by the time I started the second chapter I was hooked! I'm fairly busy so I have to admit, I didn't read it all in one sitting; it took me two! The daily life of people living so long ago are so well integrated into the storyline that I didn't even know I was learning about them! Everything just flowed. I hope he's planning a second book. Highly recommended even for older adults who like to read stories that make them feel young at heart.

— Rich Sobel
Biologist, musician, composer, author

I was fascinated by this coming-of-age story. The writing flows easily from chapter to chapter, with a narrative that can easily appeal to readers of all ages. The design of the book and its typography were a perfect fit. The artwork by Eric Carlson adds beautiful visual support to the narrative.

— Robert MacNevin
Senior drafting technician, book designer and layout artist, musician

I loved the book and the illustrations. I enjoyed it as an adult and want a copy for the kids as well. The emotions of Sev, the protagonist, are complex but recognizable as he grows and faces his own doubt, skepticism and fear. Interwoven within the narrative is subtle learning for young and old readers on the geography, ecology, culture, diet and secret societies of his times.

— Kirstie Overhill
Physician, parent

I couldn't put it down and neither could my daughter. *The Eyes of the Leopard* is a triumph of historical fiction, bringing to life a time rarely written about, with the detail and nuance only an archaeologist of Brian Hayden's calibre could provide. Don't miss this read. Share it with every schoolteacher, child and amateur archaeologist in your life. They will thank you for it.

— Manda Aufochs Gillespie
author of the *Green Mama* series of books,
founder of Folk University and passionate YA book club leader

It is a wonderful story with a message that hopefully will be heard by many young folk.

— Paul Gitlitz
Musician, composer, teacher

This is a strong story. I found the hunting scenes in the early chapters really cool. . . . Very different from how things work now. . . . They put a lot of pressure on their kids but made them strong too. They taught them tons of things and skills it would be interesting to learn.

— Nicholas Hayes
Fifth grade student

My son Nicholas finished it, devoured it really, and then reread it.

— Jack Hayes
Parent

It was very hard to put the book down once I started reading it since it tells you what things would have been like before. I liked the map of the Bear Clan territory and how it described all of the places that you could go. I want to read it again! I hope another book like this one will come out.

— Eloïse Wilmsen
Fifth grade student

My boys were captivated by the first chapter, begging for more as I read it aloud. *The Eyes of the Leopard* was a great family read for us to enjoy together. I imagine this unique story will be read again by my boys on their own as it delighted their imaginations.

— Serene Watson
Parent

The Eyes of the Leopard

THE EYES
OF THE
LEOPARD

BRIAN D. HAYDEN

Illustrations by Eric Carlson

GRANVILLE ISLAND
PUBLISHING

ISBN: 978-1-989467-42-8 (paperback)
ISBN: 978-1-989467-43-5 (ebook)

Illustrator: Eric Carlson
Book editors: Aislinn Cottell and Lisa Ferdman
Copy editor: Marianne Ward
Cover designers: Omar Gallegos and Arlene Hayden
Book designer: Omar Gallegos
Map: Jamie Fischer

Granville Island Publishing Ltd.
105 – 1496 Cartwright St.
#14354, Granville Island
Vancouver, BC, Canada, V6H 4J6

604-688-0320 / 1-877-688-0320
info@granvilleislandpublishing.com
www.granvilleislandpublishing.com

For my children and
grandchildren, and all those
who are curious children at heart

CONTENTS

MAP OF THE BEAR CLAN TERRITORY

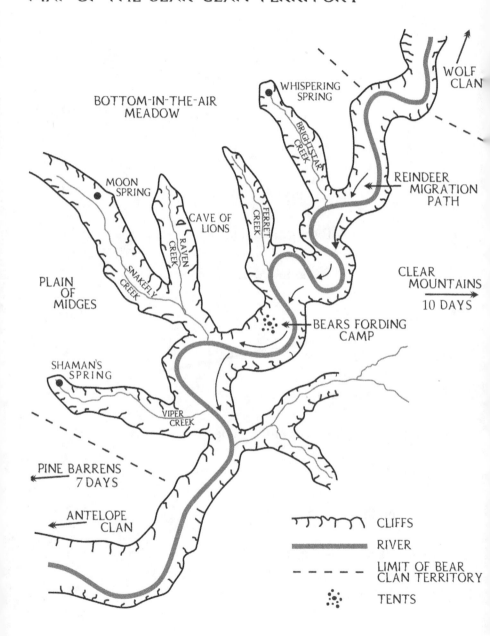

THE DARE

TWENTY THOUSAND YEARS AGO, IN THE ICE AGE
REFUGIUM OF SOUTHWEST EUROPE, STILL LUSH WITH
GRASS PLAINS AND FILLED WITH ANIMALS

The three boys in buckskin tunics watched the hare's movements from their hiding place behind the thicket of blackberry bushes. Holding his breath, Sev slid his father's net out of his tanned hide bag. Nearly thirteen cold seasons old, he squinted his brown eyes, trying to appear sure of himself.

"I'll hold this end," he whispered. "Runt, you drag that end over to the rocks. Then, Aros, you can chase the hare into the net."

"No," said Runt, hunching his rounded shoulders. "I'll use my spearthrower. I've got good aim. This is good practice for hunting big game, like reindeer. And you don't know the hares around here — they'll run any which way. Drop that dumb net!"

"I won't." Sev tried to keep his voice down. "I've been in Bear camp territory for three cold seasons now. I *know* what hares will do."

"Quiet, you two!"

Sev's eyes flicked toward Aros at the unexpected outburst. The tallest of the trio, Aros had an easy air of confidence that Sev admired. He was usually taciturn, his deeply set brown eyes watching from behind a shock of black hair. When Sev looked back at the hare, its head had lifted.

Their prey pricked its ears in their direction and scampered away.

"See? He heard you," Aros said flatly. "No meat for tonight . . . again."

"What've you got against using a spear?" Runt grabbed a flint scraper from the worn and discoloured bag at his hip, a bag that had been discarded last cold season by a family in better circumstances. He began sharpening his spear's wooden tip with irritated strokes. "A maggot would get more meat than you hunting with your oh-so-perfect net, or anything else."

"That's not true!"

"Yeah, yeah, yeah. What've *you* ever killed? I've never seen you come back with a mammoth or an aurochs, not even a reindeer or antelope!"

"I'm not afraid of using a spear!" Sev straightened from his hunting crouch and brushed away a few strands of hair that had fallen over his eyes. It was getting long, but Sev liked the feeling that he was less visible to others. It helped him avoid their attention when he didn't want to be involved in things.

"Nothing bigger than a rat," Runt continued. "And who knows how you killed that. Maybe a bear stepped on it. No wonder your family was starving when you came here from the lowlands."

"There isn't any big game around here! I'd get one if I went farther out."

"You don't have the guts to go where the powerful animals are. Are you afraid of offending their spirits? You scared that a stupid hare's spirit will come back to haunt you? You're just talking big . . . big empty. All your daydreaming won't even catch a mouse."

"I'm not afraid," Sev insisted.

So what, if I don't look like a mighty hunter and I like to think things through before lunging at an animal. That doesn't make me a coward.

"Don't tell me you're not afraid!" Runt drew himself up to his full height, his cropped head of reddish hair barely coming to Sev's slender shoulder. "You never even go near the sacred places. You'd never dare go," he paused and lowered his voice, "into the cave where the animal spirits are."

"That cave is sacred," Aros interrupted. "You could be killed for going in there without permission."

"What? Why would they kill someone just for looking around?" Sev said.

Runt glared at Sev, freckles seeming to emphasize his eyes. "If you're so brave, why don't you find out and tell us? *If* you get out alive."

"Fine. Where is this scary cave, anyway?"

"Runt doesn't know," Aros said. "We've never been allowed near it. It's the Cave of Lions."

"We know the trail heads off from Snakefly Creek and then up Raven Creek," Runt began.

"Shh!"

"Don't shh me!"

As they argued, the boys turned away from the meadows where the tall grasses brushed their legs. They headed back along the trails through the willows and aspen of the creek bed, toward the Bear Clan's encampment by the river. The cool evening air of the late warm season flowed down the mountains from the distant ice fields and across the rich grass steppes into the river valleys, threading through sparse pines on the slopes and down along the flood plains of willows. Gradually, it cooled flushed faces.

Sev had listened in silence to his age-mates bickering. Even after three cold seasons in the Bears' camp, he still sometimes felt like an outsider. Runt and Aros had known each other all their lives. He sometimes worried they only let him tag along because Sev and Runt were the last in the clan to join the unmatched men and boys — too old to stay with their parents, but not old enough to establish their own family. They only got together occasionally to do things. And they'd never mentioned the Cave of Lions before. Sev's jaw tightened.

"I want to know what makes the cave so sacred. I want to see it for myself."

Runt stopped walking, his eyes widened. Even Aros looked alarmed.

"Sev—"

"We'll do it tomorrow." Sev cut Aros short. "You both have to come along and watch me go in. We can go after we eat something in the morning. Then we'll see who the *real* scaredy birds are!"

CHAPTER ONE

THE FORBIDDEN PLACE

"I thought we were going together!" Sev scowled, opening out his hands.

"We never agreed to that. And *you're* the one who says there's nothing to be afraid of," Runt shot back, his green eyes shining with challenge. "No animal or ancestor spirits. They're just stories the Elders tell to keep us from seeing what's hidden in the cave," he said, imitating Sev.

"The Elders are leaders for a reason. They know things we don't." Aros frowned. "I don't feel good being even *this* close."

The older boy took a couple of steps back and looked up at the pine and fir-covered hillsides of the valleys to where

Raven Creek joined Snakefly Creek. Sev followed his gaze as the shrill call of an eagle echoed down the valley, its distant silhouette floating high above the canopy.

"Sev, they could come after you for this — if something in there doesn't kill you first. Maybe you just want us along so the Elders don't think this was your idea."

"It *wasn't* my idea." Sev glared. "It was Runt's idea, remember?"

"I knew you didn't have enough stomach to go up there on your own." Runt smirked.

"I'm braver than both of you, I don't need to go into the cave to prove it! But I want to see what's inside. I'm sure the Elders won't do anything to me just for peeking."

"Bring back something to prove you went in," Runt said. "Aros and me, we'll stay here."

"Fine, I'll go alone. But if anybody comes near, you give a raven's call to warn me. Promise?"

Aros and Runt hesitated, then nodded.

Sev turned away from them and walked steadily up the path along Raven Creek. He looked back only once, before he was out of sight. The other boys were sitting down on an old fallen tree, heads close together as they spoke.

A hundred paces up, the path narrowed into a ravine. Sev followed the faint track upward, weaving among the aspen and pine trees that now scattered the slope. In some places, the path had filled in with pine needles, making soft treading for his bare feet.

Doesn't look like anyone comes up here very often.

As he went, Sev carefully looked over every outcrop of the grey limestone, but there weren't any obvious gaps — and the path continued on past them.

Eventually, he came around a corner and saw a larger outcrop, bordering a marshy section of the stream where a stand of birches reached for the sky. He faltered, his heart beginning to race as he spotted a dark declivity in the rock face. The entrance was higher than he could reach, framed by bulges and boulders of grey stone that thrust through the ground at the sides.

He'd only taken a few steps forward when his attention was caught by a muted rustling sound. Something was in the bush, about twenty or thirty paces off to the right of the outcrop. He scanned the undergrowth anxiously. The shuffling noise came again, closer. Sev froze, breathing lightly so as not to stir even a tuft of eagle down.

Maybe there really are spirits in places like this.

A branch snapped, and a slim grey paw appeared at the bottom of a bushy juniper, twenty paces from Sev. Before he could take another breath, the full body of a hare appeared, ears pricked high.

Sev smiled.

"Nice day, brother hare. Maybe you can send me some good luck if I don't go after you?"

Whiskers bobbing as it munched on a mouthful of greens, the hare looked fixedly at Sev, then hopped back into the bush.

Sev relaxed his stiff pose and returned his gaze to the cave's entrance. After thinking about what to do for a moment, he moved away, back down into the ravine. He needed some torch sticks.

Flint thunderstones were best for cutting wood. He picked up two rocks that looked promising, but when he tried to knock an edge off each, he found that they'd been fractured by frost and immediately broke into useless pieces. Maybe making the torch sticks out here wasn't such a great idea after all, but he'd wanted to avoid any probing eyes back in the encampment.

He had better luck with his third choice. A blow with his hammerstone revealed an undulating pattern in the rock, like low ripples on water. That was good thunderstone. He carefully aimed the next two blows and was satisfied with the keen edge they produced.

Scrambling up the side of the ravine, he found a pine that had been previously cut on one side.

Probably by the Elders who used the cave.

Drops of amber seeped from the gash, flowing over dried, crusty, older sap. The fresh droplets reflected the Sun like the Shaman's beads, and Sev couldn't help reaching out to touch them. They stuck to his fingers and smeared when he tried to wipe them off with his tunic. Rubbing them with dirt helped, but tacky spots remained on his hands.

Sticky wolf piss!

He turned back to the tree. Using his newly made chopper, he began to strike along the edges of the gash. The stickiness on his hands improved his grip on the stone, he realized. He gouged out four deep grooves in the pine's trunk. Tossing the sticky chopper to the ground, he stretched his cramped hand.

Next, he found an old, fallen, hard juniper branch and cut it in two, making sharp wedge-like ends on each segment. Sev rammed the wedges into the grooves in the pine and, after pounding them in with a large rock, managed to pry out four long lengths of sap-soaked wood. He laid these aside and slipped off his shoulder bag.

The fire kit that he carried consisted of a rod, a flat slab of aspen wood and some fine wood shavings. Setting down the aspen slab, he carved a small depression into it with a stone flake and positioned the rod straight up in the groove. He spit into his palms and began to twirl the rod between them, steadily increasing the pressure and speed as his hands repeatedly worked down the wood and returned to the top. The friction rubbed off most of the remaining sap on his hands.

Eventually, a thin line of smoke rose from the growing mound of wood powder at the end of the rod. Soon, the smoke began to billow. The muscles in Sev's arm ached by the time a small red ember appeared, no bigger than the eye of a fly.

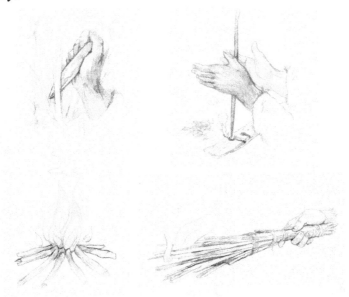

Placing some wood shavings on top, he blew on the precious spark, which glowed brighter and brighter until a red tongue leapt up. With the flame, the rising swirls of smoke dispersed like antelopes attacked by wolves.

He gathered a few twigs and larger juniper branches to add to the fire. They smelled sweet and musky as they burned.

You never know, if spirits really do exist and really are here, this smell should make them happy.

Just to be on the safe side, Sev rummaged in his bag for two round white starstone pebbles and a few flicker feathers. Digging a small pit near the cave's entrance, he laid the offerings inside. After covering them again he pressed his hands against the earth and addressed the looming rock face. His voice quavered.

"Spirits of the cave, I am Sev, son of Ené. I come in peace, to learn your ways. I leave these gifts in respect, and I ask for safe passage."

Returning to the fire, he lit three of his newly made pitch sticks, bundling them together in one hand. The fourth he tucked into the cord around his waist. He heaped dirt over the fire to extinguish it and hid the blackened spot with dry leaves.

I wonder if anyone saw the smoke?

He paused to listen. There were no warning calls from Runt or Aros.

It would have been a lot easier if they'd at least come this far to help out. But no, they're too pigeon-hearted to do anything like that. Anyway, I managed well enough without them.

He studied the mouth of the cave. Almost twice as tall as he was, it looked like the maw of a giant enraged bear, ready to swallow him.

Maybe this isn't such a good idea after all. Spirits are one thing, but what if there are bears or hyenas inside? It's probably too early for bears to go into caves for the cold season — but you can never be sure about hyenas. And how did the Cave of Lions get its name? Maybe I should have asked about that.

Turning the pitch sticks to keep their ends lit, he approached, eyes wide, staring into the blackness. Tensing his jaw, he took a step into the dim light of the maw, then another. As he advanced, the gentle caress of cool air slid across his face, as though the cave was breathing. The floor smelled of decayed stone and damp clay. The recesses of the cavern had never known the sun.

Sev held his torch well off to his side to avoid being blinded by the light. His giant shadow played on the stone walls like an immense restless spirit, its form and movements jagged, jumping back and forth with the flicker of the flames. At first, he was disturbed by the shadow image, then entranced. Could there be animals, monsters or spirits lurking in the utter silence behind the huge chunks of stone that had fallen from the cave's roof at some point in its eternal existence? Everything around him oozed a sense of ancient timelessness.

Farther in, the flickering of his pitch sticks revealed strange, frozen shapes cascading down the cavern walls. Farther still, the roof lowered, and long, bony fingers hung down from it, wet and shining. They seemed like icicles but made of some kind of white crystal, or stone. Drops of water clung to their tips.

This was a completely different world, a world of dreams, like the images in deep springs that dissolved with the drop of a pebble. But these dreams were frozen, utterly unreal. The silence, too, seemed unnatural. It was total, broken only by the occasional *plip* of water falling into a pool somewhere deep inside the cave.

Sev reached above his head and broke off one thin tube. As he turned it over in wonderment, cold water drained from inside the broken end. He tasted a few drops. They had a trace of chalky tartness.

Wait until Runt and Aros see this!

With great care, he wrapped the treasure in a scrap of antelope leather and tucked it into his bag.

Moving on, he noticed red dots marked along one wall. Mystified, he moved closer. The floor was wetter here. Clay oozed up between his toes, leaving deep tracks. Crouching down, he saw other footprints in the clay. He pondered the sizes and lengths of the toes and arches but recognized none of them.

They look recent.

As Sev slid his feet sideways to obliterate his own tracks, the light from his pitch sticks sputtered. He rubbed their tops against the wall to knock off the accumulated charcoal, and the flames sprang back to life. They illuminated a stark black handprint on the stone, inches from his face. His heart jumped.

Higher up, the flame revealed the red painted head of an aurochs, a wild bull. Before Sev could examine the drawing, a high-pitched shriek sounded from somewhere deep in the cave ahead of him. Another shriek came, and another, the echoes creating a clamour unlike anything he had ever heard. His knees turned to limp snakes, his mouth suddenly dry as dust.

Is it the spirits? Are they coming for me?

He stood, keeping as still as the rock formations around him, holding his breath.

Out of the darkness, a muffled whoosh descended toward him. The space lit by his pitch sticks filled with movement, hundreds of fluttering objects rushing through the air. They threatened to envelop him like a thick, black cloak. Nearly deafened by the ear-piercing din, Sev crouched down against the wall and tried to disappear into the stone.

Flying moles — hundreds of them!

Sev scrambled to get away. He slipped, and dropped his torch. It hissed in the wet clay and died. With the light snuffed out, the piercing screeches began to subside as the animals gradually retreated back into the cavern's depths.

Sev stumbled toward the distant, dim light of the cave's entrance. Halfway there, he tripped over a cone of stone sticking up from the floor. There was a sudden bright flash behind his eyes as pain shot through his knee. He grabbed his leg and felt warm, sticky blood.

Limping on, he finally reached the cave's mouth and burst into the late-day sun.

Gradually, his breathing slowed. His heartbeat steadied.

Bears and lions! That was more than enough for one day. He scanned the surrounding hillside. No sign of anyone. Good.

As he checked to make sure that the ashes from his fire were still covered, he felt a chill at the back of his neck. He turned.

A leopard was crouched on the outcrop above the cave.

Sev didn't dare move as the rare, powerful feline stared at him, its amber eyes seeming to size him up. After what seemed like an endless moment, it stood, calmly turned and headed up the hillside, disappearing over a ridge.

With a deep exhale, Sev broke into a hobbled jog back down the ravine.

He was glad to put distance between himself and the cave, but even as he ran, he couldn't help but think back on the strange rock formations, the flickering shadows and utter silence. The footprints, and the mysterious images on the walls. Everything was so strange.

What happened inside? What did the images mean? What lay deeper in the cave?

I have to know. Someday, I'll be back.

◇ ◇ ◇

"What happened?" Runt got up from the log as soon as Sev came off the trail from Raven Creek. "Did you fall? Is that how you hurt your knee — or did you get clawed by spirits? Did you even make it inside?"

Sev didn't answer, moving past the other boy to sit on the log.

"Prove that you went! Did you bring back anything?"

"Here, look." Sev pulled the piece of antelope leather from his bag and unwrapped the white crystal. He was surprised to find it intact — he'd felt sure that it would have broken when he fell. Still wet, it sparkled in the sunlight.

"What is it?" Even Aros seemed dumbfounded.

Sev cradled the crystal in his hands and shook his head. "They hang down from the roof and drip water. The cave is strange alright. It's got painted handprints and red dots, and animal drawings. Thousands of flying moles live there, too. They swooped down on me, but I escaped. No spirits, though. Nothing that scared me."

Runt took the crystal to inspect it, but his fingers slid on the slick surface and it slipped from his hand. It fell onto a rock, shattering into glinting fragments.

"Wolf piss! Now it's ruined!" Sev kicked Runt in the shin. "At least it proves I was in the cave. Don't tell anyone, or I'll say you went too. And we'll be enemies for life."

Aros and Runt said nothing.

Sev picked up the fragments of the crystal and threw them into the woods. "Here, give me your wrists, to prove you'll be true," he insisted. He took a sharp thunderstone flake from his bag and, seizing Runt's hand, made a shallow cut across the back of his wrist. A thin line of blood seeped up.

"Agreed? Are you sure? I know how you talk. You have to be absolutely sure about this."

Runt grimaced, but nodded. He licked his cut as Sev grabbed Aros's wrist to make another thin line, then did the same to his own. They rubbed their wrists together to mix their blood.

The other two boys stayed silent as they walked through the overhanging willows and then took a long detour around the camp in order to arrive from the upriver direction, on the opposite side of the camp from Raven Creek. Sev hoped it was enough to disguise their trespassing. People were always watching where others were going to and coming from, and they couldn't risk anyone wondering where they had been.

CHAPTER TWO

HUNTERS GREAT AND SMALL

The Sun's Follower shone through the deepening purple and blue sky, well above the thin, yellow line that now hugged the earth's horizon. It was a bright wanderer that came and went like a server at a feast — bringing food or supplications to Osti, the Great Sun, as it rose and set. The point of light looked strangely reddish tonight.

Maybe dust in the air, whipped up by the winds from the ice mountains. Dust storms sometimes choked people on the ground even far away from the glistening range. Sev picked up his pace. He wanted to be back at the unmatched men's tent before the light disappeared completely.

He descended quickly from the upland grassy meadows back into the treed valley, deftly passing between the branches of willow and aspen that hung over the path. The gutted marmot hanging from his belt flopped to and fro. It was twice as big as its squirrel-like cousins, but it was his lone catch from a full day of hunting.

Near the base of the valley cliff, Bakar, Xabi and Kip had started the evening fire in the centre of the cleared area, several paces from the tent for boys and unmatched men.

"Ah! Here comes Sev, the mighty hunter. Ah-ha-ha!" Morsels of half-chewed meat and drops of spit erupted from between Bakar's teeth. His lank frame convulsed with bursts of forced laughter. Sev looked at the ground.

"Not even a skinny hare!" Bakar's pale eyes eerily reflected the firelight. "Just a smelly, stinky marmot!" He imitated a marmot whistle and sniggered with his snub nose. "Must have taken all your hunting smarts to get it! Can't you *ever* get anything bigger? No wonder you've never been allowed in the big hunts. I bet you couldn't even bring down a reindeer if it licked you on the nose."

Sev's jaw tightened. "It's enough to fill *your* greedy belly," he snapped. "If you don't like marmot, you don't have to eat any. And I'll do more than you ever can in the big hunt next moon. You'll see."

Bakar answered with more fake laughter, echoed by his friends. Xabi's extra weight shook as he too sniggered. Kip's commentary was a knowing grin from his tanned face, shining front teeth revealed by the kink of his harelip.

Sev watched their tongues wag as they laughed and shouted — tongues like flames, tongues that seared. He retreated to the other side of the fire, away from his tormentors.

Everyone has bad hunting days. Everyone.

He took the limp marmot from his waist cord and used a stick to push aside some wood and coals from the fire, then scooped out a shallow pit in the hot earth where they had been. After placing the animal's body inside, he covered the pit with embers, ashes and dirt. Then he took some dry willow and aspen branches from the pile of jumbled sticks and placed them over his catch to build the fire back up. Even dry, the willow made a lot of smoke.

Sev's nose wrinkled up at the sharp whiff of burning animal hair, but the aroma of roasted meat soon followed as the darkness of night fell around him. Bakar's group settled down. When Sev finally pulled the carcass from the pit, it was so tender that one of its legs fell off in his hands. The fat marmot had a strong gamey taste but enough fresh meat and grease to satisfy Sev's gnawing hunger.

Mmm, done just right. Don't even need a blade to cut it.
"Sev!"

He looked up and made out Aros's tall frame approaching through the gloom, tunic flapping at the knees. His friend strode into the circle of light cast by the fire and sat down next to him. Sev shook the ashy dirt from the remaining marmot leg and passed it over. Between satisfied cheek clicks, they grinned at each other.

"So, what did you do while I was out tracking?" Sev said.

"Me and Runt went with the women to pick blackberries. But we kept to ourselves. There's some in the bucket by the hazelnuts if you want some."

Sev crawled to the tent and scooped out two large handfuls of blackberries, gulping them down with a satisfied smile, before scooting back to the fire. Aros was licking grease from his fingers.

"Is the marmot all you got?"

"Yeah. I saw some deer tracks south of camp, but they looked pretty old. They were already crumbling around the edges. No point in following them."

The two fell silent, listening to the wind whistling down the valley.

Maybe a storm coming.

The crunch of nut-cracking from Bakar and his gang created a syncopated rhythm against the fire's crackles. Sev took a handful of hazelnuts from the common pile near the tent and grabbed a couple of stones to split them open, sharing the nut meats with Aros. He watched the older boy out of the corner of his eye.

Nothing seems to bother Aros. I like that a lot. It would really be nice if we got to be closer, like clan brothers.

"Hey, Aros, would you be interested in joining with me to try tracking some game in a few days?"

"Sure, but my father wants me to go with him to visit his sister upriver in the Wolf Clan camp soon. He goes every moon pretty much, and I haven't been for awhile, so I really should go with him. I'll let you know."

"Fine by me. If you're away, I can check with Runt to see if he's interested." Sev hesitated. He wanted to talk to Aros about the cave, but looking sideways, he caught sight of Bakar. The boy was close enough that Sev could see the flash of his teeth from the fire as he talked. *Too risky.* "Umm . . . maybe we can talk some more about nets and spears tomorrow."

Aros nodded, then yawned, got up and headed toward the tent — ignoring Bakar and his friends as they erupted in jaybird squawking talk.

Trying to be inconspicuous, Sev moved closer to the fire. The smoke stung his eyes, but he wanted to overhear the other boys' conversation. It seemed to mostly involve Bakar's one long fingernail, which he fussed over as a sign of imagined special importance. Then there were the robins that had eaten the blackberries the women had crushed and set out to dry, and Xabi stepping into some fresh scats that Benat's pet wolf cub had left on the trail near camp. The talk eventually turned to the coming migration hunt, and then to the girls' and widows' tent. Sev listened more intently.

"Yeah. That Nara," Bakar said. "She doesn't talk much and seems to spend all her time working hides. But when she plaits her hair. . . . Yeah."

"I like Xana's daughter, Perra," Kip said. "She's always laughing, and that makes me happy."

"Anyone is better than Irati. I don't think she ever bathes." Bakar sniggered.

Between the lewd comments that followed, the boys held long kurkan strips of dried reindeer meat in their teeth and, with flint flakes, sliced off pieces to stuff into their mouths.

My fresh kill was a lot tastier than their old dried kurkan meat from last cold season. Lazy slugs! They don't have any right to laugh at my hunting skills.

Bakar finally noticed Sev watching them. He motioned to his friends to draw closer and spoke in a lower tone. Soon, his speech was punctuated by more laughter.

What are they planning? Bakar and his so-called friends. He doesn't care a nit about them. He just wants someone to laugh at his stupid jokes. Wait — that sounded like my name. Are they making fun of me again? Sev couldn't hear anything clearly. Frustrated, he retreated out of the smoke.

Sev's uncle, Kiré, appeared out of the night, interrupting his thoughts.

"Bright stars tonight, Sev. How did the hunting go?"

Sev gestured at the marmot's charred head and bony remains.

"I've got a friend who might enjoy some of that!" Kiré reached into his shoulder bag and extracted a slinky, squirming ball of fur.

"A ferret! Is that my father's, or a new one?"

"Your father's. I borrowed it. I'm still looking for one for myself." Kiré placed the marmot head in front of the ferret, which lost no time in sniffing and then crunching down on the treat.

"I've got a bit of kurkan that I can share with you, too." Kiré pulled a sizeable strip of the reindeer meat out of his shoulder bag and handed it to Sev, who took it and immediately sliced off a piece to chew on.

"Your father's received some good news," Kiré continued. "As you know, last moon he gave a special feast for Izar, the Shaman, and Benat, the Headman, and three other Elders. It cost him a lot of his stores and some of his prestige pieces — tusk-shell beads, antler carvings, ermine skins and fur caps."

"I didn't realize he had that much stored away."

"Last year, he gave or loaned some honour goods to several of our allied friends here and up the valley for their own feasts. Over the past two moons, he's been collecting debts from those people. It allowed him to pay for the feast for Izar and the others. So, now he's been accepted into a higher rank of the Lion Lodge. It's an important step."

"What does it mean?"

"Well, he'll take part in more meetings with high-ranking Shamans in our clan, here at the Reindeer Fording, and with important men from other clan territories up and down the valley. They've given him a new honour name: Leopard's Paw." Kiré clicked softly from each side of his cheek. "Later, he may have other responsibilities. He'll be expecting more of you now, too."

"Maybe I'll get to see him a bit more, then."

"You need to understand, Sev, that it has not been easy for him to establish us here. Food and other things can be limited. New families always seem to upset some people. Your father has had his hands full trying to gain acceptance for us. That's why this promotion in the Lion Lodge is so important."

The ferret finished its snack and wriggled its way into the sleeve of Sev's long tunic, tickling his arm. Sev giggled.

"Hey, you!" He gingerly fished it out and held its head up to eye level. "You can't stay in there. That's my space. I'll go to sleep and might roll over and crush you."

The ferret looked Sev calmly in the eye. It seemed to understand his words. With a few deft strokes of Sev's fingers along the top of its head, the animal relaxed into a satisfied ball of fur between his crossed legs. Sev sat back and watched the sparks of the fire somersault in the wind above the tent.

When the blaze began to dwindle, Bakar, Kip and Xabi crept inside, ignoring Sev as they jostled to get in. Shortly afterward, Kiré put the ferret into his bag and followed them. Left alone, Sev sighed. It certainly was difficult to be accepted here. He watched the black night encroaching on the dying fire and felt a prickle of unease, as the image of the yawning dark cave flashed in his mind.

Just how special can that place be? Hardly anyone ever talks about the Lion Lodge or what they do. They just tell you to stay away, or to watch their ceremonies and be grateful. When you ask what goes on or why you have to stay away, they just close up tighter than a fist. It's strange.

We didn't have anything like that with the Fox Clan back in the Clear Mountains. Things were simpler there. Our Shaman was a little odd, it's true. But maybe that's what happens when you talk to the spirits all the time. Anyway, he was a lot more friendly than Izar, even if he didn't have any fancy beads and pendants.

Ené seemed to care more for us then, too. Now, he's always busy doing other things.

Sev used to be close to his father, who'd taught him how to make long darts and often taken him spearfishing. Sev had loved it when visitors came at night and Ené would tell stories about animals or ancestors or the stars. It had seemed a more carefree life in the mountains.

I wish we were back there.

Getting older certainly had its difficulties, too. Boys who could begin to hunt even marmots had to leave their family tent and live together. And it was a bad draw that put him in the same tent as Bakar. He would have much preferred to be sleeping in the other unmatched men's tent on the other side of the encampment. Even if he would be with Runt, it would be far away from Bakar. But at least here he was with Aros and his uncle.

The boys' and unmatched men's shelter was made of twelve reindeer hides stretched over a branch frame that made a short cone, larger than most of the family tents. Despite the size, everyone had to pack in tightly, so it was always warm inside.

A chill had caught his neck, and the whine of mosquitoes was distracting his reverie. He got up and stood for a while beside the tent listening to Urtzi snore inside, then he ducked through the door flap. In the darkness he felt, more than saw, the larger masses of Kiré and Urtzi sleeping in the middle. He knew that Bakar, Xabi and Kip had their sleeping robes on the right side of the two men. Sev squeezed into the space on the left, next to Kiré and Urtzi, where Aros was already dead asleep.

He closed his eyes, trying to ignore Urtzi's snorts. Years ago, before Sev's family came, the older hunter's wife, Ametza, had disappeared while out alone collecting hazelnuts. No one talked much about it, but Sev had been warned that it could be dangerous to venture into the more remote areas of the Bear Clan's territory. Individuals and even small families camping in isolated areas had occasionally disappeared. No trace of Urtzi's wife was ever found. The men who'd followed her tracks through the trees had apparently noticed signs of a scuffle, but the trail had ended abruptly at a massive rock traverse. The trackers concluded that she had probably been taken captive as a wife or slave by rogue hunters from the Pine Barrens, near the sea. Since then, Urtzi had rarely spoken. Without any children of his own, he had moved back to the unmatched men's tent and hadn't taken another wife since.

Sev turned over. He was glad to have his buckskin tunic to sleep in on this cool night; the leaf-fall season was fast approaching. And he was glad to have his uncle separating him from Bakar. He frowned. It seemed like the older boy would do anything to make fun of him. Sev couldn't understand it. He shuddered to think what Bakar would do if he found out about Sev's venture into the cave.

CHAPTER THREE

BITTER RIVALS

"Ooo-waaaah-eee-eh," Sev intoned, eyes closed in concentration.

"Hurry up, dummy!" jeered Kip. "Your sour singing won't help you."

He opened his eyes. Kip was larger than him and moved with exaggerated gestures that made him seem even bigger. *Probably to compensate for his harelip.*

"You're chasing away your spirit helpers with that awful chanting," Xabi chimed in. "Hurry up and choose!"

Sev studied Xabi, who was holding his pudgy fists behind his back. Xabi never seemed to think on his own. He was always mouthing the same words as Bakar. It was probably

Bakar who told Xabi to play against Sev, and even which hand to hold the toka piece in.

The light of the grease-bowl lamp played on Xabi's tanned skin and cast flickering shadows on the walls of the crowded tent. Sev frowned, then pointed.

Xabi drew his right fist forward and opened it to reveal the toka, a small crystal, a sunstone, its clear facets glinting.

Kip and Bakar hooted low in disapproval. Aros and Runt cheered. Sev picked up Xabi's two rabbit skins and a stone spearpoint, to add to his pile of winnings.

"Enough of this child's play!" Bakar pushed his way to the centre. "Time for a real toka match. It's all or nothing, mouse-hunter!" He flung down ten rabbit skins together with a handful of spear points, and glared at Sev. "You guessed which hand the sunstone was in. Now it's *my* turn to guess."

There was a stir in the tent as Aros and Runt gathered close around Sev while Kip and Xabi stepped back to huddle with Bakar.

"High stakes!" whispered Sev, covering his mouth with his hand. "You've got to help out by distracting Bakar any way you can. Make it hard for him to concentrate. Grunts or jibes, anything. We'll split the winnings afterward."

"I'll do my best cave bear grunt," Runt said.

"I've got a pretty good jaybird squawk," Aros offered. "They might think it's one of them squawking."

"Great! I'll try to block his spirit vision with my chant. Let's go."

Both groups broke up and jostled for viewing positions. Kip went to the entrance flap behind Sev. "First, a quick pee."

"Let's see how good your spirit helpers are against mine, O great hunter of mice!" sneered Bakar. "Or maybe you don't even *have* any spirit guardians! Judging by your catches, I'd say you don't. Your puny standing and skills aren't worth protecting anyway. Go ahead. Hide the sunstone."

Sev resumed the customary chanting and shuttled the sunstone from one hand to the other behind his back. Then he closed his right hand over it and stood with his fists behind his hips. He cast his mind about, trying to think of something unrelated to the game. A forest of stone icicles flashed before his eyes. Sev caught his breath for a moment, before he swiftly replaced the image with the memory of his mother giving him his first shoulder bag.

Behind him, Runt and Aros hooted and cawed, but Bakar remained calm — almost smug.

Something isn't right.

"The stone is in your right hand," Bakar said confidently, after a deliberate pause.

Sev grudgingly extended his right fist and opened it to show them the sunstone. He stole a glance at his rival. Instead of grinning triumphantly at Sev, Bakar was beaming toward the entrance wall of the tent. Sev followed his gaze.

There was Kip, standing a small distance behind Sev and flashing a smile back at Bakar. Sev saw him quickly retract the finger that had been pointing at Sev's right hip.

Rigged! Bakar's nothing but a cheat and a thief!

Sev exploded. He threw the sunstone in Bakar's face and lunged. "You stinking piece of dung! You cheating louse!"

He grabbed Bakar's arm and twisted it sharply. Bakar kicked Sev's feet out from under him and they both went down. Sev's jaw slammed into the ground. Pain shot through his face. He pulled Bakar's hair and bit into his arm, but only found buckskin tunic. The others yelled and jeered.

Bakar managed to get up onto his knees. He delivered two hard blows to Sev's side, then one to his head.

Everything blurred.

Then strong hands were gripping him from behind. He was dragged out of the tent, onto grass under a nearby grove of willows. His head was throbbing. He tasted blood and dirt.

As he lay on the grass, his heavy breathing eventually slowed. The cool night air was soothing on his face, and the rush of the river in the distance was calming. But his ribs ached. In the moonlight, he saw his tunic was smeared with dirt and charcoal. He fingered the bottom edge where a number of fringes were missing.

I hate Bakar! Bakar and his whole rotten gang. Why do they follow that idiot, anyway?

Tears sprang to his eyes. He didn't know whether they were from pain in his body or his feelings of hurt and embarrassment.

An arm wrapped around Sev and gently helped him to sit up. He blinked away his tears. It was Kiré. His uncle must have been the one who carried him out of the tent.

"What was the fight about?"

Speaking thickly through his swollen lip and painful jaw, Sev slowly related the evening's events. Keenly aware of his uncle's close attention, he took care to hide the fresh cut on his wrist.

"You have to be careful when you gamble at toka," said Kiré. "It's a serious matter. A man can lose all his wealth, even his children. Some go so far into debt that they lose their own freedom."

"I only lost because Bakar cheated! He's been mean to me ever since we came here. It's been three cold seasons! I don't know how to make him stop."

"Listen, Sev. Don't let him bait you. Let him play his little games, trying to impress his friends by making others look dumb. You need to spend *your* time practicing your skills as a hunter, or a carver, or a trader. Or finding a spirit ally."

"I'm trying! But I don't have anything to pay for special training for any of those things. Rabbit skins don't amount to much."

"I'm sure your father will help you with anything you can't acquire on your own."

"I don't think my father cares *what* happens to me!"

"Of course he does. He cares very much. He's just busy making sure that our situation is secure here and that you have enough to eat and wear. And he's needed in the band council, and now in the Lion Lodge too. The spirits favour your father. They'll continue to make him successful. If you develop your natural talents and inner strength, they'll favour you, too."

"Maybe. I just—"

"Sev, you have all the qualities that you need. Bad things happen in everyone's life. You have to learn to deal with them. Bakar's just a braggart who's been spoiled by his father. He doesn't have your abilities. You need to take a higher path, one that might put you in touch with the Sky World some day."

"I don't know if I can do that."

"You can. You're clever and a keen observer. You're already on your way to becoming a good hunter. Just sharpen your skills and people will treat you with respect." His uncle put his hand on Sev's shoulder. "You should rest for a few days and recover from this fight, but then you should start thinking more seriously about the future."

Sev was too exhausted to talk any more. Seeming to sense his mood, Kiré didn't offer any more advice. They sat in silence looking at the stars, listening to the distant rush of the river. At last, Sev rose to his feet. Leaning heavily on his uncle, he walked to the sleeping tent. They settled off to the side, away from Bakar and his friends, who had already lain down for the night. The pain in Sev's jaw deepened as he tried to get comfortable.

I hope Bakar's really in pain. It'd serve him right. Next time, he won't get away with his putrid tricks. I'll throw them in his face. The slug.

Over the following days, Sev nursed his jaw and lip, avoiding Bakar as much as possible. He felt moody and irritated, even brushing off Aros when the other boy offered to take him up on the hunting trip he'd proposed. He felt relieved that Runt hadn't come around as well. In fact, he hadn't seen Runt for an unusually long time. *Probably busy scrounging leather scraps for patches.*

He didn't sleep well either. His dreams were filled with the sound of dripping water and painted hands, and he'd woken several times in the night convinced he was still inside the darkness of the cave. What if the Lion Lodge did find out? How severe could their punishment be? What could they do to him?

One evening, when the bruises on his face had largely healed, Sev went to his father's tent. A faint glow shone through the reindeer skin walls as he approached. Outside the door, he called out.

"Hey-o. Greetings inside. It's Sev. May I come in?"

"Hey-o. Certainly. Enter," his father's voice replied. Sev pulled the entry flap aside and stepped into the light of the small, warm space. His mother, Yana, sat close to the small stone bowl in front of Ené that served as their grease lamp, its two burning wicks casting a soft shine on her face. She was wearing her plain, daily tunic and was deftly working an awl, bone needle and sinew thread upon a half-sewn pair of fringed buckskin leggings in her lap.

His father's second wife, Asha, sat in a darker part of the tent by the entrance plying a hide with a bevelled bone to soften the buckskin.

"Hey-o. Greetings, Mother. Greetings, Father. Greetings, Asha."

"Greetings, son Sev," said Yana. "My you are growing fast! Your uncle, Kiré, is obviously taking good care of you."

"He is. I'm glad that he's staying in our tent. He's a good guide." Sev cleared his throat.

"In fact, he recently suggested that I should start thinking about acquiring some training. But that involves wealth payments, and I don't have any wealth to speak of. So, he suggested that Father might be able to help but also said that Father, now Leopard's Paw, had just used much of his wealth to advance in the Lion Lodge."

Sev turned to his father, sitting cross-legged on a mat opposite from the tent entrance. He was wearing his plain tunic. His shaved cheeks left a short beard on his chin and a long mustache, making him look very dignified. "And I meant to congratulate you on your new honour name when I entered."

"Thank you, son Sev. Yes, it is true. I did use much of my wealth for my promotion in the Lion Lodge. My brother is sometimes overly anxious to see family members establish themselves. Myself, I think it is a bit premature for you to begin thinking about training, especially with the wealth payments required."

Ené paused, tilting his head.

"It would be more prudent to wait another year or two. It may take a while, but I would eventually like to see you obtain a position of some status, and that is what training is for. But it does take wealth. If you are going to be getting into scraps with other boys," Ené paused again and raised his eyes, looking at Sev with his head still tilted, "you'd better try to improve your standing. What kind of training are you interested in?"

Sev squatted down and haltingly told his father about the snide comments the other boys made about his hunting skills and how he never was able to bring back anything bigger than a hare or marmot.

"Ah, well, the best hunters are in the Wolf Clan, upstream from us where there are no good fordings. The so-called hunters here in the Bear Clan have been spoiled by the easy kills during the great migrations and the communal hunts. You may have to live with the Wolves to train for hunting, and that would mean more payments. Next year, I'll see if it can be arranged. Until then, you should keep practicing your trapping and your aim with a spearthrower. Is there anything else that interests you?"

Sev paused before answering. "I've been thinking it might be useful to learn the high language, the one that you use when important people from the faraway clans come trading, or for ritual events. Or — it might be good to learn how to make nets or carve animals," Sev added as an afterthought.

"Hold on. That would be a lot to undertake. I don't have time to teach you myself, but we may be able to find someone with the knowledge of carving and net making. Learning the high language takes more arranging. I would need to ensure that there are no objections from others in the Lodge, and I need to better secure my position before I can do that. "

Rising, his father stepped to the centre of the tent where there was good headroom and rested his hand on Sev's shoulder.

"But I can tell you some of the most simple words in the high language, like 'shosho', which means 'goodnight'. In fact, I am very tired now, so would ask you to return to your own tent."

Sev tried to hide the heavy sadness in his eyes. He was relieved that Ené's back was turned to him.

"Thank you, Father. I appreciate your help and I hope to make you proud of me someday. Shosho."

He exited into the night.

Wolf piss. I guess it's not going to be that easy.

CHAPTER FOUR

THE FALL

O ne Moon later, during the Blood Moon, Sev sat at the boys' and unmatched men's tent, sharpening the wooden tip of his spear and waiting for the sound of the aurochs-horn trumpet. He could just see the lookout, standing high atop the majestic limestone bluffs that overlooked the willows and aspen in the river valley — cliffs that curved down into white overhangs above the river, carved out by earlier flood waters. Vertical black streaks stood out amidst a background of weathered grey rock, where uncountable seasons of rain had run down from above. Across the cliff face, a few brazen shrubs clung fiercely to miserly, crumbling ledges.

Sev had done his best to avoid Bakar since the fight. Aros and Runt seemed to be avoiding him in turn; Sev hoped it was only because of his own sour mood. He'd tried to take his father's advice and spent a lot of time by himself in the upland grasslands, but though he often saw grazing saiga antelope from afar, he could never get close enough to throw a spear.

Baroo-o-o-o. Baroo-o-o-o-o.

After another two quick strokes, Sev tossed the flake scraper into his bag. Sliding the thrusting spear over his shoulder, he grabbed the backup spear he'd made earlier and headed for the river.

The horn trumpet sounded again. The reindeer herd was travelling fast. Other hunters were running through the meadow toward the river, their stone knife sheaths flapping on the waist cords wrapped around their buckskin tunics, spearthrowers in hand. Each man carried bundles of long darts, all tipped with sharp stone points.

Bear cousins from downriver clambered into canoes. They had agreed to paddle upstream and wait for the reindeer to enter the water. Meanwhile, allied Wolf Clan visitors from upriver positioned themselves below the fording, ready to dispatch wounded animals and catch any floating dead ones. Though their assistance was welcome and would be rewarded, the Bear Clan hunters would keep the renown and benefits of killing the most reindeer for themselves.

Away from the river, near the treeline, Sev's sister, Osane, was piling more firewood onto the stack that had been prepared to dry the butchered meat. Nearby, Sev's mother and Asha were tying the last poles to a drying rack. Bakar's mother and Xabi's mother were constructing similar racks by hearths farther along the treeline.

Sev counted seven firewood piles in all, each belonging to a separate group of allied families. At the edge of the meadow, he spotted the antlered headdress of Ekain, the hunt coordinator, who was directing hunters to their assigned positions.

Ekain turned and motioned to Sev. He hurried over.

"You have spears? Good. Can you help to dispatch any wounded that make it downstream?"

Sev nodded eagerly. "I'll do my best."

My first reindeer hunt!

"Good. Go just below Xabi. He's stationed a little below the fording, where the river cuts a deep meander."

"Where?"

"See, where the bank is undercut and some willows are falling into the water?"

Sev's gaze followed Ekain's finger over the meadow, along the river, into the trees lining the bank. "I think so."

"Make a blind there. Hurry! The main body of the migration will be hitting the fording full force any time now. And stay clear of the hind legs, even if one is down."

Sev dashed across the meadow and entered the woods, well back from the river. He passed Bakar and Kip crouching behind a log, a half dozen spears piled between them. As he neared his assigned position, he spotted Xabi's backside nestled in the brush at the top of the riverbank. Stepping carefully, he continued on as quietly as he could, darting behind tree trunks.

Xabi doesn't need to know I'm nearby. He's nothing but trouble.

Sev chose a concealed spot behind a thick rose bush near the bank out of Xabi's line of vision but with a good view of the river. He broke some branches from young willows and stuck them into the ground around him to better disguise his position. Crouched behind his makeshift blind, he kept as still as possible. All thoughts were now on the hunt.

The woods around him fell silent. From his vantage, he couldn't see the other hunters, but Sev knew that they were there, maybe fifty in all, including those who had journeyed from the allied Bear cousins and Wolf Clan. They were waiting, hidden behind brush or crouched in canoes under the drooping branches hugging the bank. The only sound was the rush of water over the rocks at the ford. Sev wondered how many reindeer were destined to travel to the spirit world that day.

A light haze of dust was rising to the tops of the willows, up from the far riverbank. A few moments more and Sev could see some branches rustling, just where the river bent upstream and went out of sight.

They're getting close.

A few antlered heads poked out from among the bushes. The animals entered the water cautiously — these were the forerunners, following the herd's accustomed trail. The hunters in the canoes let them pass.

More and more reindeer began to appear, surging into a massive throng that pushed forward, those behind forcing those in front out from the forest and down the bank.

It's like a waterfall of animals. They're so tightly packed, I bet I could walk on their backs across the river!

At first, they advanced undisturbed. He listened intently for the din of a thousand hooves, like far distant thunder, scarcely audible above the noise of the river.

Baroo-o-o-o. Baroo-o-o. Sev's heart jumped. The main body of the migrating herd had reached the river's edge.

A volley of long darts flew from their spearthrowers, and reindeer began to fall.

They hardly even have to aim!

As the hunters began to move in, Sev saw some of them point to specific reindeer in the water, hitting each target with their long darts to show off their prowess. The river was dyed red with blood.

Behind Sev, the surviving animals ran panic-stricken along the age-old migration trail through the trees.

Xabi's figure rose from behind the bushes ahead, his plain tunic bulging at his midriff. He aimed at two panicked animals that were swimming past, trying to escape the slaughter. Both his attempts missed their targets. His spears floated away downstream.

A small young buck was headed for the bank near Sev. As it hobbled onto shore not seven paces from him, he saw a dart embedded in its side, oozing blood. Sev held his breath and waited until the buck turned its head away. Then he rose silently from his blind and threw his spear with all his strength. It hit the wounded buck between the ribs. The deer took two paces, then collapsed. It was a quick kill.

Moving quickly to the body, Sev's heart pounded as he withdrew his spear. Careful to avoid the animal's still-twitching hind legs, he bent down close to the bull reindeer's head.

"Go to the Father Reindeer. Go to the prairies of eternal green. Go and ask for a new body, so that you can return." He stroked the reindeer's forehead as the light left its eyes. With a final gasp, it stopped breathing. Sev paused to catch his own breath, then dragged the heavy load into the woods away from the river.

Back at his blind, Sev watched other reindeer sweeping past, swimming in the red, red river. Shifting his gaze, a different movement caught his attention, higher up above the bank. Xabi's full figure was slowly making its way along the trunk of a willow that had partly fallen into the water. His bare toes slotted around smaller branches that reached toward the sky, giving him purchase.

He must be trying to get a better shot.

Perched precariously at the end of the trunk, Xabi raised his arm sharply and launched his last spear. Body twisting to compensate for the sudden motion, his feet slid. Arms flung into the air in a vain attempt to regain balance.

The splash as he hit the water was lost in the bellow of panicked reindeer. Sev couldn't hear his cries over the din, but he could see Xabi's mouth moving as his flailing hands grasped frantically at the air above the water. Every time his mouth opened, it filled with water.

Sev looked around wildly, but all attention was on the hunt. *Nobody else saw him fall. And the canoes are all upstream! Xabi can't swim. Wolf piss! There's no one else to help him. And I can't swim either!*

Sev scrambled out from his blind.

Scanning the bank, he seized a fallen willow sapling on the ground nearby. Dragging it to the shore, he waded in as far as he dared.

Xabi was being swept downstream. As he neared where Sev stood, he made an effort to catch a small branch that hung down into the water, but his reach wasn't long enough. He went under.

Sev stared at the swirl where Xabi had been. A moment later, the boy's head came back to the surface, sputtering. Sev extended the willow sapling, digging his feet into the silty river bottom to withstand the deep current's pull.

"Xabi! Grab onto the branch!"

Xabi turned his head toward Sev, saw the branches of the sapling and reached out again. His fingers fumbled around the slick leaves, then slid off. The effort plunged him back under.

Sev stared and waited. Finally, he spotted a moving shadow beneath the ripples, but it was farther downstream. He pulled himself back to the bank and rushed through the woods. He saw Xabi's round head come up, then go under a third time. It didn't reappear.

Sev searched the churning water, eyes straining. He kept going, fifty paces, a hundred, and then backtracked. Nothing.

He went farther, to the next bend, where the river had cut cliffs into the limestone hills. The bank grew narrower and

narrower, until it ended with sheer rock plunging into the water. He couldn't go any farther.

Even this far down, the water was still tinted pink with blood.

CHAPTER FIVE

AFTER THE HUNT

The lookout's final blast on the aurochs horn indicated that the last of the herd's stragglers had passed through. The hunters shouted out a resounding "Kai!" in response.

The climactic cry was followed by an eerie silence, broken only by the ever-present rush of the water at the fording shallows, a kind of little death of exhaustion after the intensity of the hunt. Sev looked over the dry grass interspersed with occasional withered and trampled wildflowers, faded and fallen oranges and yellows. He watched flies land on the darkened smears of blood spotting the fur of the reindeer he had killed. They darted away as he moved his hand near.

His legs ached. The image of Xabi's round face being dragged under the water seemed engraved on the trees and

AFTER THE HUNT 41

in the sky. It appeared in the grasses and on each stone he passed. It was everywhere. If he had just extended his branch another handspan or two — but he had strained as much as he could. Or had he? It weighed on his spirit far more than the young bull reindeer weighed on his efforts as he dragged it across the meadow.

Even if I never liked him, he didn't deserve to die. He was the same age as me! It's not right. I wonder if his spirit will stay around the river? What if it decides to haunt me?

Sev stopped to rest his strained muscles and to look at the panorama before him. Smoke rose from the fires that were being lit, the hunters stood silently by the kills they claimed. Many reindeer bodies still lay out on the bank of the river and scattered over the meadow by the fording. The entire hunt had lasted only one handspan of the Sun's passage through the sky, but the herd seemed far larger than it had the previous leaf-fall season. The hunters had used all their long darts before the last reindeer crossed the river.

Two men moved past him, lugging a large bull reindeer by its antlers to the first fire where the women had prepared their butchering area. Sev scanned the crowd for Ekain's antlered headdress and then resumed dragging his own bull through the meadow.

After only a short interlude, the space was soon animated. Everyone was immersed in a task: hunters hauling and rough butchering their kills, the older children carrying firewood and the younger children searching the fields for broken or lost dart points. The women had already begun cutting thin fillets from the larger joints of meat. Sev looked on it all coldly. He felt detached from the world, as though everything was unreal.

Sev found Ekain dragging two smaller reindeer toward the fires. He left his own prize and hurried to catch up to the hunt coordinator.

"Uh, Ekain."

"What is it?" Ekain did not slow his pace. "Why aren't you helping? We've got a lot of work to do, getting all these animals butchered, filleted and dried."

"I, uh — I killed a bull, down where you told me to set up."

"Good. Can you drag it to the clearing, so the women can fillet it?"

"Yes, I was, but I — I need to talk to you. Something happened down there."

Ekain stopped and turned to face him.

"Well? Tell me."

Sev spoke slowly. He told Ekain how Xabi had thrown spears at the swimming reindeer and missed, how he'd then tried to get closer by stepping along the trunk of the fallen tree. How he'd slipped and fallen in the river. He told him about the willow sapling and how he saw Xabi go under.

"The idiot!" Ekain's jaw muscles tightened. "Did anyone else see it happen? Does anyone else know?"

"I don't think so."

"I'll tell Xabi's family. But it will have to wait until we get these animals taken care of." Ekain placed his hand on Sev's shoulder. "It wasn't your fault. You did what you could. Go see to your kill."

As Sev looked around, it all seemed dream-like. Everyone was busy and intently focused on the tasks at hand, but the only sound was the river. He approached the first fires and the butchering areas around them. He saw a few hunters pointing at and counting the carcasses they'd claimed. He knew they were calculating how much meat the kills would provide for their families in the cold season and how much would remain for trade. Any hides not used for clothing or tents could also be traded. He looked at the heaps of limp reindeer. There were too many for Sev to even estimate their number.

Sev struggled to bring his bull the last few paces to the butchering station where his mother, his sister, and Asha

THE EYES OF THE LEOPARD

were working with Aros's mother and sister and two other families. His father and Kiré were laying one carcass after another behind the stack of branches.

"Sev, is that yours? I'm so proud of you!" His mother beamed. "What a splendid haul!"

For a while, Sev watched Urtzi as he skinned each reindeer, cutting down the belly and along the legs with a stone blade and then detaching the skin from the body by using one hand to punch between it and the muscle. Even in his daze, Sev was amazed at how quickly the old hunter worked and at how little blood ended up on his aged tunic.

Kiré was pulling tendons from the animals' legs with a stout stick that he drove into their ankles and then used as a lever. His uncle grimaced, red-faced, as he strained to loosen the strong sinew from its attachments to muscle and bone. Aros's older brother, Eneko, disjointed the reindeer into portions of leg, head and back, cutting the ligaments at precisely the right places and snapping off the ribs with a sharp-angled block of stone. His tunic was spattered with blood. He gave the biggest cuts of meat to Sev's mother, sister Osane, and Asha, to slice into thin fillets for drying to make kurkan for the cold season and for trade. The women were much cleaner in their work, often rinsing their hands and stone knives in a bark bucket of water.

Sev looked down the line of butchering stations. The fire tended by Bakar's and Xabi's families was at the far end of the meadow. People there were smiling and joking as they worked. He saw no sign of distress.

I guess Ekain hasn't given them the news yet.

Yana looked up. "Sev, take the lungs and guts in that bark tray and toss them into the river. And bring more firewood. See if you can find some dry poplar branches. Osane, go with your brother and take the bucket to bring back water."

"I can go by myself," said Sev.

"Your sister's going with you. We need more water."

Sev lifted the bark tray, piled high with intestines, lungs and other offal. It was heavy and awkward, but he managed to grapple with it and headed off. He could feel the warmth of the organs even through the bark. Osane grabbed an empty bucket and ran to catch up with him.

"I thought you'd be happy to join the hunters," Osane said. "You don't look happy."

"Leave me alone."

They reached the river. His sister filled her bucket while he dumped the guts into the water a little farther downstream.

"Here. Take the tray back with you. I'm going to the woods to get firewood."

"You're being mean!" Osane sniffed, grabbed the tray and headed back.

Sev spent as long as he could collecting wood. On his way back, he could smell the rich aroma of livers, hearts and kidneys roasting. They had been placed on the coals of the slow fires beneath the strips of meat drying above in the smoke. He dumped his load of branches onto the pile next to their station. His mother was washing her hands and her blade knife in the bucket.

He watched the meat cooking on the fire.

"Can I have some of the meat that's roasting?"

"Take the ribs. The other parts are for the hunters."

"I *am* a hunter."

"No. The real hunters."

"Can I have some ribs, too?" pleaded Osane.

"You'll have to wait. Your brother dispatched one of the reindeer, so he gets some first."

Sev gnawed on a few ribs and watched Urtzi again, now knapping off long blades from a large core of thunderstone. He passed them over one by one to the women to replace their dulled filleting knives, which he then took and resharpened, using an antler tip to remove small flakes from their dulled edges.

The hunters and butchers, his father and uncle among them, paused occasionally in their work to help themselves to the choicest cooked morsels: tongues, liver and cheek meat. They clicked their own cheeks in approval and exchanged accounts of their kills.

Although delicious, the succulent ribs did little to dispel Sev's gloom. His mother had to ask him repeatedly to dispose of the offal as it piled up and to fetch more wood.

"What's wrong, son?" she asked finally. "This is the most important day of the season. You brought down a bull! You should be excited — yet you look like a bison sat on you."

Sev didn't reply. He couldn't rid himself of Xabi's eyes, wild with panic the moment before the river swallowed him.

As dusk darkened into night, Yana declared that the smoldering fires didn't give enough light to let her cut the meat properly, and building them up now would only burn the fillets. She and the women sat down to eat and feed any children that hung around their fire.

At the neighbouring fire, the visiting hunters from Wolf Clan boasted and mimed the day's events with animated movements. Their greased and ochred faces were made even ruddier by the firelight.

Just as Sev was considering heading to the tent, there was a sudden uproar at the end of the meadow. Sev could barely discern Ekain's antlered headdress amidst the gathered figures. A piercing cry came, followed by a heart-rending wail.

It's got to be Xabi's mother, Baca.

After several long moments, Sev saw Ekain leave that fire and approach each of the other fires in turn. The laughter died as he went.

Xabi's mother and her sister continued wailing well into the night. The usual singing and animal dances were replaced by hushed conversations and long silences, with only the rushing of the river to disturb the stillness.

CHAPTER SIX

UNCERTAIN GROUND

Early the next morning, Sev and the other boys resumed the dumping of offal into the river and the fetching of wood and water. Every family's stores of provisions were bursting with large bundles of dried kurkan. As Sev returned to the meadow from his father's raised cache, he saw Ené and Xabi's father, Yurok, approaching.

This can't be good.

"Sev, my son," Ené said solemnly. "Xabi's father and I would like you to tell us exactly what happened yesterday at the river."

Sev hesitantly recounted again what he had seen. As he spoke, he felt tears swelling in his eyes, the numbness from the previous day no longer protecting him from the emotion.

The two men nodded silently and departed.

Sev's stomach churned.

What if Xabi's father didn't believe me?

He tried to busy himself again with the firewood, but he couldn't rid himself of the dread that overwhelmed him.

Sev could barely move his limbs or raise his eyes from the ground, yet he was jittery and spooked at every shout or loud noise that came from the camp. With each trip, firewood near the camp was harder to find and he had to trudge farther into the forest, but he was grateful that it took him away.

Despite the hunt's remarkable yield, the feasting was much less festive than usual. The continual wailing from Xabi's family tent permeated the air. Kiré told Sev that no one wanted to offend the family by displaying any joy. Xabi's family seemed to be drying only the bare minimum of meat for their cold season needs and clearly did not plan to do any feasting or trading.

Toward dusk, after another intense day of butchering, drying and hauling, Sev's father sought him out. He carried a bundle of dried reindeer meat under one arm.

"Sev, I know that you did your best to save Xabi and that it weighs heavily on you. But you need to show that you care." Ené put his hand on his son's shoulder. "Here, take this kurkan bundle to Xabi's father. It will be a show of respect and sympathy. It may help to smooth things out for you."

Sev couldn't refuse. He threaded a slow path along the outskirts of the fires, trying to avoid as many people as possible.

At the edge of the woods, he slowed. An unfamiliar girl was walking the path toward him, carrying a large load of firewood. She looked at him intently as she drew near, and Sev found himself mesmerized by her sky-coloured eyes, framed by twists of dark hair. White tusk shells were sewn like Sun rays around the neck of her tunic. His stomach fluttered.

"Do you — uh — do you need help? With the wood, I mean?"

Stupid question! She's already so close to the fires it doesn't matter. And I'm carrying this kurkan.

"No. I'm used to carrying wood." She paused. "What a lot of reindeer your clan got yesterday! You must be pleased."

"Yes. I speared a big bull reindeer downstream, by myself." Sev cleared his throat. "I haven't seen you before. Where're you from?"

There was a movement, behind the girl, and Sev's throat tightened. Bakar was coming along the path toward them.

"I'm from Luku in the Pine Barrens, near the great water."

"That water sounds like an impressive thing to see. I've never been to see it. I've never even seen any big water. We came from the opposite direction, the Clear Mountains where the Sun rises."

"Well, I guess that means that I'm from where the Sun sets. I came here with my father to visit his sister and to help put up meat from the hunt. My father's a trader. He hopes to get a lot of pelts here in exchange for the mammoth ivory, seashells and visionstones we brought."

"What's your name?"

"Lorea. I'm from the Elk Clan. What's yours?"

"Sev. So you'll be here for a few more days?"

She nodded, shifting her armload of wood to rest on her hip. Out of the corner of his eye, Sev saw Bakar walking wide of them. He tried to focus on Lorea. She was smiling shyly.

"My father's waiting for me at the fire, but maybe I'll see you later?"

"And I have to take this dried meat to another family. I'll look for you at the celebration in a few days, after the butchering and drying are done."

He moved to the side to let her pass, turning to watch as she left.

Lorea.

Suddenly, the ground was rushing up to meet him. He hit hard, the bundle of dried meat scattering.

"*So-o-o* sorry, Sev. I didn't see you! You oughta pay more attention to where you're going." Bakar stood right behind him. "What did you drop? Is that meat for Xabi's family? So they'll forgive you for letting him die? You bag of dung. Maybe *that's* what you were doing around the cave: casting spells so that Xabi would fall off that tree."

"I *didn't* let him die! I did everything I could to save him." Sev stopped his reply short as he caught the full sense of Bakar's words. "What do you mean, me being around the cave? What cave?"

"Don't play dumb. You know very well."

Sev's mouth went dry. "Don't go spreading those kinds of stories, will you. They could get me in a lot of trouble."

Bakar gloated. "You'll have to wait and see."

Before Sev could speak, he heard a clatter of falling wood from behind Bakar. Then Lorea was there, thrusting an angry finger at Bakar.

"Hey! What in the Sky World are you doing? Why did you just do that? What kind of a hyena are you?"

"Stay out of it, little girl," Bakar shot back. "This slug just let my best friend die. Pick up your twigs and go to your own tent."

Lorea looked at Sev, then back at Bakar. She hesitated, then turned and retreated, picking up her load of branches.

Bakar spit on the ground next to Sev and left.

Sev got up as quick as he could, brushing off his tunic. He knelt to gather the fallen kurkan. Picking up the last piece, he looked up to see that Lorea was standing not far off down the path, looking straight at him.

Burning with humiliation and rage, he spun on his heel and sped off.

Bear dung Bakar! What does he know about the cave? And how?

Sev's gift to Xabi's father was accepted coldly.

CHAPTER SEVEN

ULTIMATUM

By the fourth day after the hunt, the number of flies around the butchering area had become intolerable. Everyone worked feverishly to finish preparing what they could — the meat that had not already been smoked and dried was beginning to smell bad and would have to be abandoned. Sev could see white maggots beginning to squirm in some pieces.

A large area of the meadow was carpeted with skins, stretched out and pegged to dry in the sun. Antlers and grease bones were piled up behind the fires, for use later in the cold season or for trade.

Sev's mother and Asha continued to tie up the last of the family's dried meat in birchbark bundles. Sev and Osane made trip after trip to their father's raised cache to store them, along with the sinew, antlers, dried hides and the many good marrow bones.

"We've got enough for almost two cold seasons," Kiré declared. "Lots to spare for feasting and trading."

But Sev's thoughts were not on the abundance. While packing up another load of kurkan, he took advantage of being alone with Asha.

"Um, Asha. You're from the Bear Clan, right?" He took a breath. "I was wondering . . . whether you know much about the Lion Lodge. I've heard vague things — how important the things are that the Lodge does, mostly. But no one seems to want to talk about them. I just want to know more . . . to be a better part of the clan."

Asha took a moment to scan the area around them before crouching close beside him.

"Listen, Sev. You're right, people don't talk much about them. But they bring the reindeer to us and ensure that the Sun comes back. They cure people who are sick and avenge those who have died from our enemies' sorcery. They have charms to protect our warriors, and they speak with our ancestors. And they are powerful. But if they suspect that someone is talking about them disrespectfully, they can find ways to hurt you. They have spies who let them know, too. I'm only telling you because we are family and alone, but the trees have ears, so I can't say much more." She grasped his hand. "Take care of yourself."

Sev stayed silent as she gathered up her own bundle and moved away. He couldn't get rid of the unease in his stomach.

How could Bakar know? We were so careful to cover our tracks. Did someone find my torches in the cave?

There's no way they actually kill people, is there?

Sev finished his tasks as the Sun was setting and went off looking for Runt, finding him on the path to his boys' and unmatched men's tent.

"Runt. You told someone about the cave, didn't you. That's why you've been avoiding me."

"Uh . . ." The other boy wouldn't look at Sev in the eye. "Not really."

"What do you mean, 'not really'? I was worried your loose lips might get me in trouble, but you swore to keep it a secret, didn't you? Did you tell Bakar?"

He glared at Runt's blank, downturned face.

"No. Not really."

"What the lion's ass does 'not really' mean?"

"Well . . . Bakar and Kip cornered me. They asked me if you were the one who lit the fire by the cave. I didn't say anything. I think they already knew."

"Great! So when you didn't deny it, that's all they needed. Who knows what'll happen now!"

"But I didn't *say* anything!"

Sev strode off, hot as a boiling rock. He went back to the meadow. Staying off the paths, he kept just inside the trees so that he could see the people around the fires but no one could see him. He had to find Bakar. He searched for the bigger boy's thin silhouette, but in the darkening dusk, it became harder and harder to make out any individuals. After a while, Sev gave up. *Maybe he won't tell anyone and just hold it over my head for the rest of my life. At least that would be better than dying.*

But when he arrived at the unmatched men's tent, Kiré was waiting for him. He spoke tersely.

"Your father wants to see you right away."

They walked briskly and silently to Ené's tent. Sev's father was alone when they entered. They seated themselves across from him, next to the flickering grease lamp.

"Son, you're in grave trouble."

Sev stared at the ground.

"The highest ranks of the Lion Lodge are convinced that you lit a fire near the Cave of Lions and went inside.

Your tracks were found there. Surely you know that it is forbidden to trespass into the sacred places here. Why in bear's madness did you do it?"

"People have always just told me to stay away. They never said why, or anything. Aros is the only one who ever mentioned anyone getting hurt for going in." He swallowed. "I thought it was just a story to frighten children."

"No! They are deadly serious prohibitions!"

Sev couldn't speak. Studying him, his father continued, "Not only that, but Bakar's father, Raven's Eye, has spread the rumour that you purposely let Xabi die without trying to help him. Everyone knows that you and he were not friends. And Bakar's father has a lot of wealth and loans. He has considerable influence in the Lion Lodge."

"But it's not true! I *did* try to help! I *told* you what happened!"

"Unfortunately, whether it's true or not makes little difference to what people think. And some suspect even worse. They claim that you used powers obtained from the cave to make Xabi slip and drown. If enough people believe this, you may have to run — to find some place far away, with family members willing to take you in. The Lion Lodge has powerful members in all the bands in this area, so you'd have to go very far to escape their reach."

Looking down to avoid his father's eyes, Sev managed a few difficult swallows.

"I was out hunting with Runt and Aros, and they started making fun of me. They said that I was afraid of hunting and of animal spirits and things." His face burned. "I know I shouldn't have gone in, but I just wanted to prove I wasn't a coward."

Ené's tone softened. "If you did not intend any disrespect, maybe you can still prove yourself instead of running. The Lion Lodge could kill you as punishment for trespassing and as a warning to others. However, if they think you could be useful, they could put you through an initiation ordeal. It would be very difficult, but if you survive they may accept you as a young member. I am still a junior member myself, and there are some high-ranking men who do not favour me. I hope that other members will prevail in our favour."

After a few moments, he added, "Paying for your initiation would require rich offerings. I've just given much of my holdings to the Lodge. But I still have the Blade of Eagles, which is very valuable. It was made by Xantri, the most famous of all stone knappers, and it took me five years to acquire all the furs and tusk shells to purchase it. I was going to save it to arrange for a high-placed marriage for you, but if they agree to initiate you, this is more important. Even giving such a precious item to the Lodge for your initiation, I'll have to borrow quite a bit. But I don't mind having to pay back debts for many more cold seasons — that is, if the heads of the Lodge are willing to accept you."

"Can't you explain to them what happened?"

"Son, once you've trespassed on sacred ground, you're subject to the Lodge's whims. If you stay here, they'll either kill you or initiate you, no matter your age."

Sev felt a sudden tightness in his chest.

If I have to run, where could I go? I could try to live by myself in the mountains. But that would be a huge risk. I don't know if I could survive. I still can't kill much game on my own. It would be either that or stay in hiding among strangers and away from my family for the rest of my life.

Maybe they'll let me join the Lion Lodge, but that sounds dangerous too. Even if my father can pay for my initiation, what if I don't make it? I could be dead either way.

In the turmoil of his anxiety, another thought occurred.

What if I never see Lorea again?

CHAPTER EIGHT

MISTS OF THE MIND

*F*our toes spread in a wide arc with no claws — a leopard for sure. Maybe the same one that was at the cave. They're so rare, there can't be many around here.

Sev grabbed his buckskin shoulder bag from the ground and straightened up. Standing alone on the soft black earth of the trail, he gazed out over the cool, lush upland prairie. After a restless night thinking over everything his father had said, Sev needed to get away.

He was debating whether he should bother going back to the Bear encampment at all. He had left with everything he owned of importance in his shoulder bag. He could go on to

Nahia, his father's sister, who'd gone down the river when she married into the Antelope Clan. Maybe she could provide links with her husband's family that would enable him to travel even farther — far, far away from Bakar, the Lion Lodge and all his problems. He was sure of good hospitality at his aunt's — at least until they heard news about him, but maybe even after that. He should be able to reach her encampment before sunset, so no need to take food. There would be some hazelnuts along the way to eat.

If he was going to be blamed for Xabi's death, he would be an outcast no matter what, even if he was initiated into the Lodge. Bakar would be unbearable, even Runt and Aros might stop talking to him. Dying on the tundra all alone would be better than enduring that kind of life.

But then, what would his disappearance do to his father, the rest of his family? Would they become outcasts too, having harboured a son who appeared guilty of all accusations, having run away without defending himself? A coward. Then there was another consideration: the slim possibility that if he returned to the Bears' camp, he would be able to meet Lorea again and explain to her that he wasn't at all responsible for Xabi's death. That he'd tried to save Xabi. That thought was far brighter than the other, gloomy outlooks.

Osti, the Sun, descended toward the distant mountains ahead of him, glinting off their white peaks. A flock of ravens passed overhead, eyeing something on the ground and cawing amongst themselves.

Probably squawking about a carrion feast. Maybe the leopard's kill. One of the ravens turned its head to stare at him. Sev stared back.

Past him now, the birds sped in front of a low cloud bank that was creeping across the sky. It looked foreboding. *Maybe rain.* He stopped for a moment to consider his tenuous decision a final time. Then, mind made up, he turned around. He would go back on the trail, back to the camp of the Bears before it got too dark.

The air was chilling down as Sev descended the slope from the prairie back into the treed valley. Muck oozed up between his toes in the wet parts of the game trail. In the valley, clouds billowed lower, misting the top of the tree canopy. Farther still, wisps of vapour flowed through the bushes and swirled around his footsteps.

Sev raised his arm to keep the overgrown branches from hitting him in the face. The mists seemed to twine around his legs and rise to his head, cooling the air that he breathed. Sev looked up. Grey fog engulfed the tree branches and hid the setting Sun. Sev tried to make out the path through the thickening mist. He looked back from where he'd come, or what he could make of it.

Maybe not such a good idea to come out alone so close to sunset, not at this time of year. But who knew such dense fog would form so early in the season?

Every step took Sev into denser mists.

Wolf piss! Nothing to see even two paces away in this mess! Can't recognize anything, not even the Sun. I can hardly see the trail!

There was no way to tell which fork of the trail to take back to camp, and dusk was gaining on him. Shapes were dim and vague. Everything was still except the rustle of the bushes as he pushed through them.

A dark mass loomed before him, more felt than seen. In a few more paces, Sev could make out the blurred, rounded form of a limestone cliff face that disappeared into the dusky fog above. A few paces along the base, he came to an overhang. Inside the rock shelter, charcoal bits and old thunderstone flakes littered the ground from previous visitors.

It was no use trying to return though the mists. Hopefully the other boys and unmatched men wouldn't be too worried if he was gone for just one night, especially given the fog. He began to search the brush nearby for firewood.

With a jerk of his head, Sev tossed a shank of hair out of his face and rummaged in his buckskin bag for his fire drill kit. Flint scrapers and flake knives fell out with the flat slab of wood and rod. He wrapped the knives in a scrap of chamois leather and shoved them back in the bag.

Even after the fire had started, Sev felt unsettled. Night had come, and his stomach complained about the lack of food. His hunger turned his thoughts to the time of starvation that his family had known back in the mountains, when the animals had just disappeared. The younger men and older boys of their clan had gone off on raids to steal dried meat from raised caches in distant, unfriendly territories. Sometimes they were successful. Other times only a few of them returned, some wounded.

After two cold seasons of being half-starved, they had exhausted all possible food sources, even trying to cook and eat old buckskin. Sev's father had resolved to move closer to his sister, Nahia, and the clan that she had married into, the Antelopes down the river from the Fording. The Antelopes were having a stressful time themselves and were unwilling to admit any more people, but the Bears had more resources and agreed to let him join their camp.

Both Sev's grandparents had died during the starvation time. He had few memories of them, but he recalled their wrinkled faces. His grandmother had taught him how to let the Sun open green pine cones, then knock them against rocks to make the seeds fall out. His stomach rumbled. The roasted pine nuts were so good. And his grandfather had often taken him hunting for ducks with their nets.

I hope their spirits came with us.

Squatting with his back to the shelter wall, he tucked his hands behind his knees to keep them warm and watched the fog forms flow past his meagre, flickering fire. He could hear distant noises, maybe falling branches or squirrels searching the leaves. Maybe something bigger. There was no way to know for sure.

He imagined shadowy forms, just beyond the edge of the light. Forms that prowled slowly, silently, vague faces staring at him. He thought he saw yellow eyes that caught the light, but then it was only a slightly brighter patch of mist. He rubbed his strained eyes. There seemed to be people walking toward him. Was that his grandfather? Did he want to tell Sev something? But then the shape transformed into a bear, standing on two legs, before dissolving into a formless mass like clouds in the sky.

Despite his anxiety, as the fire faded, Sev's eyes closed.

He woke sometime later with a start. He was under the entrance overhang of the Cave of Lions, and something was prowling around him, a long shadow. Ominous groans and cries echoed from the dark maw behind him. He kept himself flat on the ground, covering his head with his arms as the flying moles streamed out above. Whether it was just a moment or more time that passed he couldn't tell, but he finally dared to raise his head from his arms.

The dim light before dawn was progressively brightening the sky. There were no flying moles above him and no cave entrance at his back. He listened intently but could no longer hear any strange cries. He was still at the limestone overhang. Only his soul had wandered to that other place.

The sky above was a clear, dark blue now. The mists were gone. Between the branches above, Sev could still see the Sun's Follower, the only remaining bright point in the sky, which would soon disappear as Osti rose in his own majesty. It felt somehow reassuring.

But as he gathered his things and set off back to the encampment, he couldn't entirely banish the presences from his visions. The thought haunted him of what might have been watching him during the night, even as he passed a thicket of blackberries and stopped to gorge himself on the sweet bites.

When he reached the tent, Aros was the only one there, seated and trying to carve a piece of wood into a bison shape using a few thunderstone flakes.

"Hey-o, Sev. Missed you last night. Where've you been?"

"I went to the uplands but got caught in the mists and couldn't find the trail back. Pretty creepy being out there at night. Is there anything to eat here?"

Aros gestured toward the communal pile of hazelnuts. Sev grabbed a handful and began cracking them to pop into his mouth.

"So, you *do* feel some kind of spirits out there," Aros said, not looking up from his carving.

"Well, I never quite said that I didn't believe in any spirits," Sev said. "But it's hard to know for sure. I mean, maybe it's just things in your head that you're imagining. You know? Like in dreams. How can you tell what's really there?"

"Sometimes I think you just have to trust what you feel. I know that I've felt some pretty strong presences, especially when Izar is drumming around the fire, or when I'm alone in the uplands. I'm really sorry that I won't be here for the big reindeer feast, but my father insists that we have to leave tomorrow night for my aunt's — he wants to be back before the cold starts. It's too bad. I always really enjoy Izar telling about the Sky People and things. I know there's something there, even if you can't see it." He lowered his voice and glanced around. "Didn't you feel that there were spirits in the cave?"

"It was spooky, for sure. Enough to turn your toes inward. But I don't really know if there were any real spirits. Maybe. I'm sure that Izar could make you feel spirits if he was in there with you. But that would be him putting things in your head."

Sev cracked the last hazelnut in his hands.

"No more nuts! I'd better go get some more for the stash before the squirrels and jays strip all the trees. Want to come?"

"Sure." Aros tossed his carving in the tent and grabbed a buckskin to carry the nuts in. As they walked the paths to Moon Spring where the nut trees still hadn't been heavily harvested, Sev summoned his courage and spoke.

"I guess you've heard that Bakar and his father are saying that I went into the cave and worked a spell on Xabi or something. Runt didn't help when Bakar and Kip confronted him."

"Yeah. Runt told me that you were pretty upset with him. But he really didn't know what to say to Bakar. You know how he is. I don't know how anyone figured out that you were there. It certainly wasn't me who said anything. I can only guess that someone recognized your tracks either outside or inside the cave."

"Maybe so. I fell inside and was scrambling to get out, so I could have left some tracks. I tried to smooth them over when I went in, it was just in leaving that I didn't take too much care." He paused. "Do you think anyone really believes that I did anything against Xabi?"

Aros was silent for some moments. "I don't know. Those kinds of accusations seem more like a game to me, a game to try to get someone in trouble. It's hard to tell what others will believe, or at least accept. Some people, like Xabi's family, might be more than willing to believe that you were responsible and didn't do anything to help him. But for most people, especially the Elders, it's harder to tell what they think."

"Aros, do you think that I did anything like that against Xabi, that I didn't even try to help him when he was in the river?"

"No. I think I know you well enough to be certain that you would try to help anyone who was in danger and that you wouldn't try to use spirits to harm anyone. Why, you're not even sure that spirits exist!"

Sev groaned as Aros started listing reasons he was sure that the spirits did exist. By the time they got to Moon Spring and filled their bag with hazelnuts, they had exhausted the topic, but Sev still wasn't convinced.

CHAPTER NINE

VOICE OF THE SPIRITS

Two nights later, Sev sat at the periphery of the crowd that had assembled around the large fire near the edge of the meadow, a blaze bigger than any of the usual family hearths. Almost all of the Bears were there together with the guests who had come for the reindeer hunt.

Sev felt jittery and unwelcome, as though everyone was watching him. What had the others been saying? Was he a coward in their eyes? Someone who wouldn't help age-mates? An irreverent rubbish boy? A mud-face?

Or worse, a murderer?

Was the Lion Lodge going to ban him from the clan? Disfigure him? Kill him in his sleep, or in front of everyone?

He didn't want to be here, but if he didn't attend the feast, he would be even more of a target and an outcast.

He fixed his gaze on the flames, past the silhouetted backs of those sitting in front of him. Izar stood in front of the fire, beating slowly on his hoop drum. The droning beat lulled Sev into an anxious stupor. He usually liked the Shaman's mesmerizing rituals. The drumming was always the same and some of the stories were familiar, though often with some unfamiliar twist.

Tonight was a special event, commemorating the hunt with guests, so there was almost certainly going to be something a little different — maybe an entirely new episode in the rich mythic cycle of the Bears. The Shaman stepped closer to the fire, his rhythm strengthening. His heavily bronzed skin was a black silhouette against the firelight. His body and his long, braided beard swayed to his beat.

Sev's eyelids had just begun to feel heavy when shrill whistles pierced the air from out of the dark. Whistles that rose and fell and intertwined in eerie, melodious, then suddenly jarring tones. They were different from any human whistling he'd ever heard.

"Ah! I hear the voices of the spirits. They are approaching!" Izar said, pausing his drumming for a moment. "Listen! Listen well. They are coming near!"

With that, a shrieking, antler-headed figure fell from the night sky and landed in the fire with a shower of sparks. Sev jumped, only just stopping himself from yelling out. Yana, Osane, Asha and the other women and children shrank back. Izar gave a loud beat on his drum, as the creature landed, and then continued his previous rhythm.

Ekain, Benat, Kiré and other men remained still and expressionless. Sev looked over to his father. Ené, too, was as impassive as a stone. So were most of the visiting hunters. Sev strove to copy them while the antlered creature danced at the edge of the fire, scattering embers and sparks. Then it vanished into the night amidst more whistles, retreating into the dark.

Where did that thing come from? Was it a spirit? I didn't see anything like that in the cave. But it had the body of a man.

Then, to a softer beat, Izar solemnly intoned, "And so it was. Zarua was the first being to come down from the Sky. He was the most powerful of the great Shamans. He could transform himself and others into whatever he wished. On sweet-smelling smoke, he sent messages to his Sky companions about the lush plants there were to eat here, the abundant animals on the hoof. These messages brought other Sky beings to earth. They were drawn by the richness that Zarua described. Eki, who could transform himself into an eagle, came."

And, with that said, he beat his drum loudly, whistles rose again and a winged figure descended from the sky. It crouched and danced, extending a wing, sweeping the assembly with a piercing gaze. Then it, too, flapped away into the darkness, and the whistles faded with it.

"Others came, like Basa, Lord of Wild Things. They brought stones of light, to brighten the world at night. They created fire."

Izar put his drum down and held two large, clear crystals above his head. He struck them together three times, producing flashes like lightning inside them. Then he threw a handful of pollen into the fire's embers. A huge flare shot up.

"They mastered fire."

The antlered figure and winged being reappeared. Each scooped up a glowing ember from the fire, which they put into their mouths. The whistles resumed. The children gasped as the pair began blowing showers of sparks into the air.

"Lesser Sky Beings followed Zarua, Eki and Basa. Because they could not find female companions here on earth, they transformed themselves into aurochs and great mammoths, leopards and wolves. This allowed them to mate and to multiply. But, in time, their children began to fight amongst themselves." The whistles faded again.

Izar tapped some branches in the fire with his staff. Sparks flew. He resumed his drumming, quieter now.

"They filled the world with their children like sparks fill the air above fires, like stars fill the heavens. These beings are still among us. Some have the bodies of bison, eagles or even cave lions. Only the greatest Shamans took on human forms. We of the Lion Lodge are their brothers. We commune with all who are in the Sky. We are at one with the spirits of the Sky, of Osti, the Sun, and Ila, the Moon. Through them, we hold the secrets of life and light and fire. Look well at the full Moon tonight! Look well at the Sun when he rises. We know the secrets of the Sky People, and how to reach them.

"We intercede with them to bring warmth, growth, fertility. We sustain you and all of life! We bring you meat and marrow grease. We bring you strong broth. We bring you roots and nuts. You are our guests. Here, eat with us! Partake of our abundance! And offer thanks to the spirits that honour us now with their presence."

At that, Izar's drum fell silent. His assistants added wood to the fire. Then they brought out birchbark buckets loaded with meat and strips of fat, gobbets of marrow, cooked cattail roots, shelled hazelnuts and bark cups of hot oily soup and cool water.

"Noble guests, please wait some moments before beginning to feast, so that we may honour the spirits," Izar proclaimed. The drumming resumed, its rhythm increasing.

"*Whoa-o-oo, whoa-o-oo.*"

The antlered and winged figures joined the Shaman in his chanting, then other members of the Lion Lodge joined in too. The sound seemed magnified, as if coming from all directions. The whole world seemed to be pulsating: the people, the fire, the air, the ground and sky — as if everything were all one being, bound by the chant.

The fire blazed more brightly. All the Bears — except Xabi's family — and all the visitors were gathered close around. The precious amber visionstone beads on Izar's chest reflected glints of flame.

Izar waved his arms dramatically, bidding the two mysterious beings to dance. Their movements brought the whistling back, and the motions resembled those of fierce animals and raptors. The eagle extended open talons toward the children, who shrank back screaming. It danced in front of Sev and seemed to fix its gaze on him, then lunged with its talons outstretched. The sharp claws came close to his face, caught the end of Sev's hair, but then slid off. Sev didn't flinch, though his heart was pounding. The eagle continued dancing on to threaten others. The antlered being thrashed its antlers in front of anyone standing.

When the dancers had gone around the fire three times, Izar bowed and spoke.

"And so it was, and so it is. Now, please enjoy our gifts."

The feasting began. Sev drained two cups of the oily soup. He wolfed down roasted meat until his stomach hurt. Finally, he sat back.

Licking all around his lips, he caught a glimpse of Lorea, seated with three girls on the other side of the fire. As he watched, one of her companions turned and whispered in her ear. Lorea looked up, straight at Sev, and broke into a big smile. He tried to make his answering smile even bigger.

Maybe she doesn't think I'm an idiot, after all! Maybe she's heard that I was trying to help Xabi — not trying to kill him.

As the feasting drew to a close, Izar stood again.

"When you have enjoyed your fill, I will go to the sacred tent to speak with the spirits. Those who wish to know the will of the spirits may join me outside the tent."

He stepped away from the fire, followed by the antlered and winged creatures, who had eaten in the darkness away from the rest of the camp.

Benat, Ekain, Raven's Eye, Leopard's Paw, Kiré and five additional members of the Lion Lodge followed Izar to the sacred tent. Rather than being round and conical like all the family tents, it was a four-sided, hide-covered structure with a small opening at the top. Though it stood well outside the ring of firelight, the structure was still easily visible in the glow of the Moon. Runt, Bakar and a few others followed at a distance. Sev hung back behind them, watching warily.

He could see Izar standing by the tent. The Shaman gestured with his arms to the stars, then pointed his drum stick at the Centre Star, the entrance to the Sky World around which all the other stars turned. Sev followed the direction of the stick, above the silhouetted tops of willow and aspen, and wondered what the Sky World might be like so far up there.

Why do all the other stars turn around that one star? Is it really a way to get to the Sky World?

In a low voice, Izar muttered, "Lo," then entered the tent alone. Everyone fell silent.

After several long moments, a barely audible, high-pitched voice began speaking from inside the tent. Sev edged a little closer. Ripples appeared in the tent's skin, intensifying until they caused the entire structure to shake. A cloud of yellowish powder burst from the hole in the top. As the incantations grew louder, Sev realized they were in an unfamiliar language. He strained to glean some sense from them and was able to grasp a few wisps of meaning — long flowery references to the Sky World, to spirits and past Elders. As the words gradually became more recognizable, the spirits declared that they had sent many reindeer to reward the Lion Lodge for its performance of powerful rituals. They had driven off the malevolent Xixain spirits from the body of Benat's new son, and he had recovered his soul and his health.

Sev's wariness eased. He was not prepared for the next shrilly intoned words.

"In addition to our blessings, we, the Sky People, accept Bakar, son of Raven's Eye, to serve us in the Lion Lodge and to learn the secrets of life and light — *if* he can prove himself worthy.

"We also accept Sev, son of Leopard's Paw, to serve us in the Lodge and learn our secrets, *if* he can prove himself worthy. They must both be prepared by the next great Moon, the Kurkan Moon, to fulfill their obligations."

The tent shook more violently.

"We welcome a new spirit who has joined us: the spirit of Xabi. We saw his fatal fall. We saw those who worked their sorcery against him and caused him to die in the waters. This was the deed of the Hyena Clan, the Hill People who live in the north, away from the Sun. Their medicine makers envy our abundance. To these enemies must your ire be directed. Xabi must be avenged!"

The tent abruptly went still. No one spoke. The penetrating voice trailed off into faint, unintelligible whispers. After an extended silence, when it was clear that nothing more would be said, the group outside drifted back to the fire.

Sev stayed behind. *At least now everyone knows that I'm not Xabi's killer, and the Lion Lodge won't blame me for his death. But why does Bakar have to go through the trials too? Everyone knows he hates me. What if I don't succeed? Is this some kind of competition to see which one of us survives?* As Sev's thoughts raced, Kiré's calm face loomed out of the darkness, backlit by the fire.

"Sev, I was looking for you—"

Sev couldn't stop the words that tumbled from his mouth.

"I'm scared! The Lodge wants me to take the initiation trials. But I've heard stories about boys who didn't come back, who stayed in the Sky World forever. Do I really *have* to do it?"

"I'm afraid so."

"They're taking Bakar too," Sev said.

"Maybe he was chosen because his father can easily pay the costs. His initiation will enrich the Lodge. Or maybe the Lodge is tired of indulging his arrogance and wants him to earn his standing in the clan, to become a man. You'll have to learn to deal with him. This challenge lets you confront him on equal footing. You'll be stronger for it. You'll see."

"If I live through it."

When Sev finally returned to the fire, Lorea and her friends had gone, but the thought of her smile somehow soothed his panic. Maybe he couldn't change his fate, but he could prepare himself as best as he could for the upcoming ordeal.

CHAPTER TEN

GATHERING THUNDERSTONES

Clear weather turned the valley into an enchanted world over the next days. The leaf-fall season Sun lit up the cottonwood and aspen so that their remaining translucent leaves dazzled like dancing yellow butterflies. The ones that had already fallen decorated the brown paths and gave off rich smells of balm. The air was cool, the sky a clear blue.

Benat had assembled five of the clan's best hunters and fighters to travel to Hyena territory, to avenge Xabi's death. The heaviness in Sev's head lifted with the prospect that he was not going to be killed outright or banished. His father's and Kiré's enthusiasm for his initiation helped, too. He felt a surge of energy that pushed him to make multiple forays into the bush. He redoubled his efforts to practice his tracking skills, snare-building and spear throwing.

If that useless worm Bakar can pass the initiation trial, then so can I. His target stump emitted a dull 'thump' as his spear sank into the decayed wood. *My bush skills are a lot better than his.*

He'd found a hare's trail and begun trapping there regularly. Bending a sapling over, he hooked it under the arm of a wood peg that he drove into the ground. Then he made a loop at the end of some supple white nettle twine. The loop was just wide enough for a hare's head. He tested the twine to ensure that, once tied to the sapling, just above the trail, the loop would slide easily. If all went as planned, it would tighten around the neck of the first hare that passed along the trail and release the trap.

He gathered branches and rocks to block alternative ways around the trail opening and smiled in anticipation of a delicious meal. Then he went to check the trap he'd set the day before.

No reason to set them if you don't check them. Maybe hunting for hares with Aros and Runt is fun, but I like setting my traps better.

The other sapling hadn't been sprung, however, so he headed off for the lower part of Moon Spring, just over the ridge and into the next valley. The stream was low now, making it easy to search its bed for good thunderstones. He liked the Moon Spring thunderstones best, with their blue and red colours.

Maybe I can add a few nice ones to my initiation gifts.

Well below the spring, he heard the chortling water. Its sound was comforting, as if the spirits of the stream were singing to him. A flutter of coloured leaves blown by the breeze spiralled down to the ground as Sev set his bag on the bank and scanned the stream's bed. Selecting a large stone, he hit its edge with a hammerstone.

Bear crap! It was riddled with cracks. He tossed it back into the stream, where it made the telltale dull clack of a thunderstone with flaws. The second cobble he chose was better. The flake rang with a 'ting' as he struck it off. The inside was almost pure sky blue.

Once he had found six good cobble-sized thunderstones, he packed them into his bag. *Beauties! These will make great tools and nice gifts.*

A few hundred paces from camp, he looked around for a place to hide his finds. A little ways off the trail, he spied a low rock outcrop with three willows at the base. Using the sharp edge of one of his cobbles, he shaped the end of a dead branch into a rough blade for digging and made a small pit between the tree roots. He threw in some dry leaves and small branches on the bottom, to prevent the stones from sticking to the ground if it froze. After dropping the stones inside and covering them with dirt, he scattered more leaves to disguise the hiding place. Finally, he moved a small log over the pit, and arranged three rocks next to a tree back on the trail.

By the time he returned, everyone had already retired to their tents for the night. The fire was dying. Sev threw a few sticks onto the remaining embers, grabbed a fistful of hazelnuts and made a meagre meal. He hand-cupped some clear water from the birchbark bowl his mother had given him when he moved out of the family tent. Then he crept into the tent and lay down near the older men, on the opposite side from Bakar.

Soon he was asleep. Winged men and animals roamed the sky of his dreams. A wolf lunged at him from a treetop, then turned into a woman with sharp teeth and fingers like claws that raked across his face.

Sev jolted awake. The world was dark — silent except for Urtzi's snores. He listened for some time, wondering at the images in his mind.

Were there Sky People who became wolves, too? Dangerous things? Why would they?

CHAPTER ELEVEN

THE WOLF

Three days later, Sev went out again. He'd decided to explore the valley and uplands around Viper Creek, hoping to find game, but had come across something very different.

He bent down to examine the fresh tracks on the trail. Four toes in a high-pitched arc with large, extended claws were clearly marked in the mud. A wolf. A male or female? Was it just passing through the valley, or did it have a den nearby? The image of a snarling mouth entered his thoughts. *The dream.* He tried to recall what else he'd seen but couldn't picture any details — just a vague feeling of anxious discomfort.

Trying to put the image out of his mind, he laid his two long darts with his simple spearthrower on the ground, reached into his shoulder bag and withdrew a piece of chamois horn from a moist clump of moss. He'd thinned it down, whittled the ends into points and kept it wet to make it more flexible. Bending the horn as much as he could without breaking it, he wrapped a length of sinew twice around the ends to keep it from springing back to its original shape. He tied the bent horn to a sapling near the paw prints. Rummaging in his bag again, he took out some fatty hare intestines he'd saved from the previous night's meal and wrapped them around the horn, then strewed the rest of the entrails on the ground nearby.

He surveyed the surrounding poplars looking for a stout piece of windfall. It only took him a few minutes to locate a suitable branch, and he set off with his new walking stick over the rough path up the ravine.

At the top, Sev smiled as he crossed the grassy meadow jokingly called Bottom-in-the-Air — a reference to the women who went there to pick strawberries. At the far end, he noticed three dark patches of fresh earth, newly dug hares' dens. Looking around, he found a stone with an angular edge, which he used to make the end of his walking stick into a blade for digging.

The first hole contained only grass bedding. When he had dug a forearm's length into the second, he reached in and felt fur. As he resumed his efforts, the chamber collapsed upon two hares that struggled to free themselves from the dirt.

He dispatched them both with quick blows from the stick. He was interested mainly in their furs, already turned white for the cold season. They could be added to the other small offerings his father would make to the Lion Lodge. He also relished the thought of a roasted hare dinner.

Tucking the limp bodies under his belt, he headed back down to the valley. There, he lit a fire to roast his catch and skinned both of the plump animals.

Maybe these pelts aren't as valuable as ermine, but they sure look nice.

By the time he had finished wolfing down one hare and the forelegs of the other, licking the roasted grease from his fingers, the Sun was hovering just a few fingers' width above the horizon. The few clouds high in the sky were portents of the coming cold season. He put the skins and remaining meat in his bag and turned back toward the Reindeer Fording, retracing his steps along the game track.

Back in the trees, he blinked to adjust to the dimming light. He was about to toss his no longer needed walking stick to the side when his eyes caught something in the dirt.

Wolf tracks. Fresh.

Sev slowed his pace and looked around warily. He hooked a long dart to the end of his spearthrower and advanced half-crouched, eyes flicking between every tree and bush.

Wish I was better at using this thing.

When he reached his snare, the nettle string had been snapped and the bait was gone. He slowly scanned the surrounding thickets in a full circle. Nothing.

Sev followed the tracks for several moments before spotting a drop of blood. A few steps farther on, he spied another drop — then another. It had worked! As intended, the sinew that bound the lure had been softened by the wolf's stomach juices. The pointed horn had then sprung apart and pierced the wolf's innards. Sev could feel his pulse throbbing in his hands and face. He'd never confronted anything as big, dangerous or valuable as a wolf.

The specks of blood veered off the path onto a narrower game trail. Sev followed carefully, avoiding any dry branches that could make noise. A single misstep could turn him from hunter to hunted.

He peered through the grey thicket of poplar trunks. Looming just ahead was a white limestone rock face, streaked with greys. Scanning the area, he listened intently, his spearthrower poised in one hand and walking stick gripped in the other. The blood spots, larger now, led toward a jumble of huge boulders that had broken off and tumbled down from the cliff above.

Sev set his walking stick, spears and spearthrower against the boulder closest to him, then scrambled up the side. On the other side, between the stained, lichen-covered limestone wall to his left and the rockfall towering over him to the right, was a narrow space. A barely audible whimper trailed out from the gap.

Sev stared past the lichens and dark stains on the rock wall, past the few branches that drooped down between the rocks, past the shrubs below. The whimper turned to a low growl. With a start, he recognized the eyes of the wolf, its grey body almost completely camouflaged in the shadows between the weathered limestone.

It was large, blood dripping from its mouth, and snarled at him as it tried to rise to its feet. Nearly lost in shadow, Sev could barely make out two small pups behind it, like half-sized ferrets.

Whoa! A she-wolf with pups. Not a good idea to get any closer. I should really wait until she's weakened from blood loss.

But dusk was creeping into the valley, stretching the rocks' shadows. This might be his only chance to bring back such a prize. If he left the wolf here, it might be ravaged by hyenas or carrion birds. He edged his way back down to the ground and retrieved his walking stick and spears. Skirting the boulder, he approached the cavity, step by hesitating step.

As he approached, the she-wolf bared her teeth and emitted another low growl. Again, she struggled to get up — only to stagger and fall. Steadily, Sev drew closer, biting his lip, his pulse thudding. The wolf's weakness emboldened him, but cold tongues of ice still shot down his back.

He could throw a spear, but his arm was shaking — he didn't trust using the spearthrower. *Plus, that might damage her coat.* He grasped his walking stick tighter, but the sweat in his hands made the grip slide.

The glint on the trunk of a small spruce tree caught his eye, where a few drops of fresh sap had formed beneath a broken branch. It was only two paces in front of him, easy to reach and just what he needed. He reached out and smeared a bit on his hands. The walking stick stuck firm in his palms.

This is good.

Another step, and another. He hesitated.

Maybe she's still got enough strength to lunge at close range. Maybe she's just waiting for me to get close enough before striking. He edged a little closer. The wolf made no move.

When he was terrifyingly close to her snarling, growling jaws, he raised the stick straight up and brought it down with all his might on her skull. The blow knocked her flat on the ground where she lay without moving. He clubbed her again with all his strength, and again, and again. Finally, arms shaking, he stopped and let his heavy breathing slow down. He watched carefully for a moment to make sure that the wolf was no longer breathing. His own courage surprised him.

Wait till my father sees this! He won't believe it!

"Mother wolf. I send your spirit this day to join with all the wolf spirits that have passed from this land. May you hunt the abundant herds in the forests of the eternal wolves. Rest well and return to us when you are ready."

He paused. His prize was far too big to carry, and he had no time to butcher it in the rapidly fading daylight — but he didn't want to leave without the pelt.

Not to mention . . . Sev took the cooked hare meat out of his shoulder bag and reached for the two whimpering wolf pups.

"Hey there. Don't worry, I'll take care of you now. I can get you meat and make sure that nothing will harm you. You'll be part of a good hearth group."

His soft words and long strokes along their heads seemed to calm them, and Sev gently placed both inside his bag, tying the top loosely to allow them air. He fashioned a rough wrapping of leaves for the hare meat and tucked the packet under his belt.

Then he turned back to the she-wolf. With his sharpest stone blade, he cut through the skin of the belly, as he had seen Urtzi do. He sliced from its throat to its tail followed by cuts down each leg. He cut through the bone and muscle at the ends of the legs in order to leave the paws attached to the pelt. He severed the neck sinews and twisted the bones until the cartilage snapped, so that the head, too, remained attached to the hide. Then he punched between the skin and the muscle to separate them. Soon the naked, headless body of muscle lay exposed.

Sev could scarcely lift the massive body. He managed to lug it between two large boulders, which he concealed with brush. If it wasn't discovered by other animals, he would reclaim it in the morning.

He slung the wolf skin, with its magnificent but heavy head, over his shoulders. The darts and spearthrower could stay there until he returned. Gathering up his things, he headed for the encampment. The fresh skin was heavy and had a pungent smell, but the walking stick steadied his steps. Even with the pelt over his shoulders, wolf pups in his shoulder bag and hare meat secured at his waist, he felt light as air. *I'm a successful hunter! A man with seasons of experience couldn't do better!*

By the time he entered the main valley, he could barely see the trail — but catching the camp's familiar smokey smell, he pressed on with new strength. Once the tents were in sight, he stashed his burden and walking stick behind a tree. Then he walked casually into the clearing near the unmatched women's fire, where Osane was playing a string game with Perra.

"Brother Sev! What're you doing here?"

"I snared a hare today and thought you might like some of the meat."

"Would I! Where is it?"

"Come with me and I'll give you some."

Osane jumped up. When they were out of sight of the others, he unwrapped the package under his belt and gave her a hind leg. She grinned in delight.

"I've got some things to give our father — things to help me get out of trouble," he confided. "But I don't want anyone to know about them. Can you go to our parents' tent and check to make sure no one's inside or nearby?"

"What've you got?"

"No, sister. I can't tell you either."

"Then I won't go!"

Sev tried to convince her, but finally he had to relent. "Alright. I killed a wolf today. I've brought back her hide and head."

"Show me!"

He led her to the tree where he had cached the hide.

"It's huge!" cried Osane. "And it stinks like rotten fish. Now I know why you smell so awful."

Sev shouldered the pelt, ignoring her remark.

His sister walked well ahead of him, carefully avoiding Asha's small neighbouring tent. It was easy to find their parents' tent, glowing from inside, illuminated by the lamp. Osane called out to announce her arrival before entering. A moment later, Ené emerged.

"Sev, come in and let's see what you've got."

Sev ducked under the entrance flap, following his father. Inside, he shifted the hide onto the dried grass strewn over the dirt floor of the tent. When fully spread out, the wolf pelt

occupied nearly half the space in the tent. Ené clicked his cheeks repeatedly in approval while Sev's mother marvelled at the thick fur.

"I've got two white hare pelts, too." Sev pulled them out for display. Against the darker wolf pelt, they looked stunning. When the pleased murmurs had subsided, he declared, "And I've got another surprise!"

Untying the lacing at the top of his shoulder bag, he reached in and drew out an animated ball of fur. As Osane's eyes grew round, Sev triumphantly produced the second bewildered wolf pup.

Sev's mother clapped her hand over her mouth. His father's eyes were bright, and he was smiling broader than Sev had ever seen. Osane dissolved into giggles as the tiny pups struggled to stand.

"Son Sev, I'm bursting with pride! How were you able to accomplish all this?"

"I'll tell you, but after everything that's happened, I need to eat. I've brought some hare."

Yana set down a bark bowl of water and some dried reindeer meat pounded with berries. She chewed some of the meat until it was soft enough to give to the pups and then took it out of her mouth to feed them. Between his own mouthfuls, Sev excitedly recounted the day's events.

"Remarkable for a boy of thirteen cold seasons!" his father exclaimed. "These will be tremendous additions to the stores I've been preparing for your initiation. But we must keep them a secret for now. It's better not to show your hand when playing the toka of life."

The next morning, Ené took the wolf hide to Nahia. Sev's aunt agreed to secretly dry, scrape, tan and curry the hide to ready it for presentation. The hare pelts could be prepared by Yana, while the wolf pups would be loaned to a more distant band to hold in reserve.

"Can't I keep one?" Osane pleaded.

"No, daughter. We'll need them both as part of the payment for Sev's initiation. We must keep them secret until then."

CHAPTER TWELVE

AN UNEXPECTED ENCOUNTER

R unt scowled as he hoisted Sev's bag along with his own, both packed with new stone knives, a net and another empty hide bag.

"Listen, Sev. I know that you think that you're a great hunter now. But no one else is around to show off to except me, and I'm not impressed at having to carry all the stuff myself just so you can impress some trees by just carrying a spearthrower and some darts."

Sev glanced at him. "Listen, Runt, you owe me for letting the crow out of the net to Bakar about my visit to the cave. Maybe you can't eat wolf meat because wolf is your mother's clan totem, but I didn't ask for your help so I could keep it all for myself. Really. I asked because you and Aros are supposed to be my friends. It's not my fault that Aros went to visit his cousins upriver, but that leaves you as the only one I can turn to for help. Listen, I'll give you the next two hares that I snare. I promise."

"I'll remind you," said Runt. "Maybe some fur trim from the hares on my tunic would improve the look of this old thing. I got it from my father's brother. It's looking pretty worn out. At least it's not as bad as the willow-bark-fibre tunics that lazy moochers wear. And wolf meat probably isn't as good tasting as hare anyway. I like fresh hare best."

Without the thrill of the hunt, the walk to the boulders where he had stashed the wolf seemed longer than he remembered. Sev picked up his pace, looking at the low clouds covering most of the sky, heralding rain and cold.

"Sev, people in camp aren't blind. They'll want to know where so much meat came from."

"Don't worry. My father will take it downriver to his sister, Nahia. She can dry the meat there. Once we've stripped it from the bones and removed the guts and lungs, it shouldn't be too heavy to carry. But don't let anyone know about it."

"Why would I?"

"No reason. But you told Bakar about the Cave of Lions, when you agreed not to."

"I *didn't* tell him!"

"Well, you let him know."

Finally they arrived at the streaked limestone rock face and the jumble of boulders. After removing the brush covering, they found the carcass undisturbed.

Runt whistled. "Woo-ooo! That wolf could give anyone bad dreams! Did you really kill it all by yourself? You didn't just find it already dead? Maybe it was killed by a falling tree, or a mammoth stepped on it."

"Don't be stupid. I told you how it happened. No mammoth, no falling trees. I'm a better hunter than you think. Give me some credit, and give me a blade."

The earth beneath the wolf's body was dark and still moist with pooled blood. The two boys gathered leafy boughs to lay the butchered portions upon, dumping the useless innards into the bush. By the time they completed their work, rain had begun to patter on the poplar leaves.

Packing the meat and the choice organs in leaves tied with bramble-bark strips, they filled their loaded cinched net and bag and headed back to camp under the wet, glistening canopy of trees.

No one was at Ené's tent when they arrived, so Sev left the meat under his parents' sleeping pelts.

"Thanks for your help, Runt. Remember, don't tell *anyone.*"

"I won't. Remember that you owe me two hares."

The steady drizzle had matted Sev's hair to his forehead. He found a fur cap in his father's tent, pulled it on and set off toward Moon Spring. His three-stone trail marker was still there. He located the cache of thunderstones, brushed the leaves away, scooped out the loose earth and stuffed the best-looking stones into his bag.

On his way back to the encampment, he was surprised to see Lorea on the trail coming from the opposite direction.

She's still here! And she smiled at me when she was sitting with her friends at the fire. She must know that I didn't kill Xabi. I still can't believe she doesn't think I'm a dung ball though, after seeing Bakar trip me.

"Lorea! So you haven't left for the Pine Barrens yet. How long are you going to stay?" *Idiot. Obviously she hasn't left yet! Is that all you can think of to say? You just made it sound like you want her to leave.*

"Hello, Sev. We'll go back some time before the snows come. My father is still negotiating. He's been playing toka too. He won a lot of dried kurkan. It'll be wonderful to have so much meat, although it means a heavy burden to carry back for me. There isn't much game in the Pine Barrens."

"Well, I would really like it if he decides to stay even longer. I was hoping that I would see you again, so that I could explain what that whole thing with that boy who tripped me was all about." Sev told Lorea about Xabi, how he had tried to save him and that Bakar was just trying to make trouble. "He's always had it in for me, I don't know why, but I promise I didn't do anything to hurt anyone."

"I understand. At the time, I didn't know either of you, so I didn't know what to think. But I've heard people talk about it since, and I think I know who to believe. I don't get the impression that you're the kind of hunter who would let someone else die." She smiled. Sev smiled back.

"Thank you. Tell me, what did you think of the Shaman's story around the celebration fire after the hunt?"

"I liked the ancestor spirits that came out of the sky. I've never seen anything like it. Your Shaman seems pretty powerful."

"Izar? Yes, he's pretty good, alright. I've been thinking about how they did it. I don't think they're spirits at all, even with the strange sounds. They looked like masked men who probably climbed up a notched pole and then jumped off the pole into the fire."

"And they know how to blow sparks from their mouths? Maybe."

She doesn't believe me.

"What do you have in your bag?" she continued.

"Thunderstones. These ones will be good for making blades, but they're nice to look at, too. Want to see?"

Lorea nodded.

Sev knelt to remove three of the stones that had the most attractive reds and blues from his bag.

"How can you tell which ones are nice inside?"

"Once you've tested a lot of them, you start to feel which ones might be good. These are some of the nicest I've found. They're from Moon Spring, one of my favourite places. I'm going to give them to my father to add to the things he's presenting to the Lion Lodge so I can be accepted for initiation."

"You're going to be initiated into the Lodge? I hadn't heard that. You mean you just pay to join? I thought everyone had to go through trials, to earn their standing."

"They do. I still have to prove myself, to show I'm worthy of the initiation. But first, the initiation trial has to be paid for. I think I can pass the test. I can already hunt and trap. I've caught plenty of hares."

Hares in snares! So what? That won't impress her. Too bad I can't tell her about the wolf. I wonder if she's heard anything more about me going into the forbidden cave. Would she think I'm brave, or just stupid?

Sev hesitated. "You can have a thunderstone, if you want."

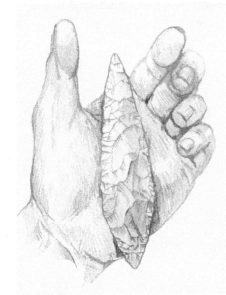

"Thanks, but I don't need one. It would only be more weight to carry."

"I can knock a blade off of one for you. That would be useful, and light."

She nodded, smiling this time.

Sev chose a core that displayed nice undulations with reds that faded into blues on its test flake scar. He examined it to determine the best places and angles from which to strike other flakes off. After he removed three odd-shaped flakes with his hammerstone, his fourth blow produced one that was sharp all around and elongated. He held out the new blade to Lorea.

"I also made a spearpoint. You can have that too, if you want."

"You're kind. But I can't use a spearpoint. On the other hand, I can use this blade to work on the skins my father gets."

"Your father must be wealthy, to travel so far trading pelts and shells. Do you have a big family?"

"No. I'm the only one. My father must have wanted a boy for a child. But I can carry a fair load. He wants to show me around so he can find a good marriage partner for me. He doesn't think much of the boys in the Pine Barrens."

They talked on, until suddenly Lorea jerked her head up and looked around.

"I'm sorry, I've been gone longer than expected. If I'm missed, my father might come looking for me."

Sev suggested that they could meet the next day if she was gathering wood upriver. Lorea agreed.

CHAPTER THIRTEEN

AN UNWELCOME PROPOSAL

That night under the waning Moon, Kiré caught up with Sev as he was on his way to the unmatched men's tent.

"Sev, come. Let's walk so we can talk privately. There's something I have to tell you."

The two wandered a short distance outside the camp and settled themselves in the grass under a few willows.

"I have some bad news. You know your father has been struggling to meet the cost of the feast and the gifts required for your initiation. The most valuable item is the Blade of Eagles, and—"

Sev broke in. "Is it damaged?"

"Worse. It's been stolen."

"Stolen? Are you sure? Maybe my father just moved its hiding place and forgot where he put it."

"No. We've done everything to find it. Your father, your mother, me, even Asha. We've looked everywhere and thought of everyone who might have come near our cache. There can be no other explanation."

Who would steal from my father? Traders are sometimes killed for valuable items, but that's by enemies or strangers while travelling. My father's not a trader, and there's no stealing among the Bears. Everyone would know.

"Could one of the guests at the Fording camp have taken it?"

"We can't think of anyone who would. And we could never prove it." There was a long pause. Kiré drew a deep breath. "You won't like what I have to say next, either.

"Bakar's father, Raven's Eye, has concluded a marriage agreement between his family and the trader family of your friend Lorea. The families sealed their pact with a feast and an exchange of furs. Lorea is now betrothed to Bakar — though there are some who heard her arguing with Edur, her father. They say she is not pleased about the arrangement."

Sev stared at the ground. His eyelids felt heavy. *We were just getting to be friends. I thought I'd have more time. I'll need to pass my initiation trial before I can even think about marriage. Maybe I should have said something to her, or to my father, or to her father. Now it's too late! Wolf piss and dung! I didn't know I could feel this bad.*

His uncle leaned over to give Sev a long, firm hug. It did nothing to lift the heaviness that now swept over Sev's whole being.

"I *don't* like it at all! I'd like to bash Bakar's head in."

"Sev, don't do anything foolish." He placed his hand on Sev's shoulder.

Kiré waited in silence for a moment, then sighed and left.

Sev remained under the willows for a long time, unable to muster the strength to return to the tent. Above him, the Sun's Follower preceded the crescent quarter-Moon by a handspan. They shone down on him late into the night, until both faded behind the valley cliffs in the pale predawn, when at last he curled up in the grass and fell asleep.

CHAPTER FOURTEEN

DISCOVERY

When Sev awoke, the Sun was already several handspans above the horizon. He crept back to the unmatched men's tent, only to encounter Bakar on his way out.

"Oh, Sev, did you hear? Your little friend Lorea decided she can do much better than you. She's mine now. She's got spirit. I like that. It'll be a challenge to tame her. Maybe smelly Irati will have you — if you're lucky!" Bits of spittle shot from his mouth.

Sev's mind was blank. He grabbed his bag, his spearthrower and some long darts and headed toward Ferret Creek.

I'll be able to think better at the creek. Just got to get away from Bakar.

He set a few snares along the way, but his stomach was knotted with anxiety and despair.

Bakar doesn't deserve her. She'll never be happy with him.

He returned at nightfall, ravenous. All his traps had turned up empty. He scavenged a few leftover pieces of kurkan in his bag, then snacked on the communal pile of hazelnuts. He couldn't stop thinking about Bakar and Lorea. When he managed to force his mind away from them, he remembered his father not being able to pay the Lodge for his initiation, and what that would mean for his fate. His head hurt, he tasted bile in his mouth from his churning stomach and his eyes burned. He went to sleep feeling frustrated and miserable.

The following day, he ventured farther still, to the upper reaches of Snakefly Valley and the surrounding uplands. Kiré had told him stories of people who went there and were never heard from again, but he didn't care.

I'd probably die in the Lodge's initiation ordeal. Maybe that's what they have planned for me. To get all my father's wealth and then let me die. I don't care anymore.

He saw no one, and no antelope or deer appeared within range of his long darts. But on his way back, he found three hares caught in his snares. One hare provided a good meal. He saved the other two to give to Runt, as promised.

As he crossed a stream, he spotted a huge blackberry patch down the bank.

These canes are long; they'd make lots of good cordage. I should collect some for Mother, she can use them to attach all the new hides to her frames when she works them into buckskin.

Peeling off the outer bark layers was tedious, but after scraping the spines off, the outer layers broke away from the inner bark easily in small pieces. The work soothed his mind. By the time he had finished, the Sun was low on the horizon. Sev coiled up the lengths of fibre, stuffed the roll into his shoulder bag and headed back to camp. As twilight deepened, he smelled the faint familiar smoke, saw the scattered flickering of tent fires through the trees.

Like stars flickering in a black sky.

As he passed a few of the raised caches on the edge of the encampment, he had a sudden thought. He might be able to learn more about Lorea's arranged marriage to Bakar if he listened to the talk around Bakar's father's tent. Laying his darts and bag under a tree, he crept through the brush as if stalking a deer until he was crouched a dozen paces behind the tent.

Raven's Eye and a man Sev didn't recognize were sitting in front of the tent by a small crackling fire, speaking in whispers. Sev strained his ears but could catch only maddeningly brief snatches of their exchange.

". . . bring shame upon him . . ."

". . . agreed."

". . . blade in the spring . . . never find . . ."

". . . twenty furs . . . my son . . . powerful union . . ."

". . . yes . . . our control . . ."

Sev's mouth went dry.

He retreated carefully, making sure before planting each footstep that there were no sticks underfoot to snap and betray his presence. Even after retrieving his belongings, he kept checking behind him, to make sure that no one had seen him.

His thoughts scattered in all directions. *So, the Blade of Eagles really was stolen! Now it's hidden . . . in a spring? Buried in the bottom or around the edge? Or did they mean they would use it in the springing-up season?*

Are they trying to humiliate my father? Why? To destroy my chance of joining the Lion Lodge? I thought Raven's Eye was more honourable than that. How dare he! That stranger couldn't have stolen the Blade without his help. But maybe I misunderstood. I couldn't hear them very well. Still, the Blade of Eagles is missing, and this would explain it.

If they meant one of our springs, which spring could they have been talking about? There are only a few deep ones around here.

Sev wasn't sure he slept at all that night. He kept going over the same questions and the same thoughts, again and again. He was still completely awake as the first faint greys of dawn appeared through the chill morning air. He got up and headed straight up the valley of Viper Creek.

It took the better part of the early morning to get to Shaman's Spring. Surrounded by poplars, the pool of water was only about two paces across. He couldn't detect any signs of disturbed ground around the bank.

He looked carefully at the dark water. There was no way to tell how deep it might be. Pulling out a small white starstone from his bag, he dropped it in the water with a small splash, then closed his eyes.

"Hey-o. Spirits of water, keepers of this flow from the world below, I am Sev, son of Ené. I have need of help to find my father's blade. Please guide my eyes, my feet and my fingers to recover what has been lost. Hey-o."

He opened his eyes, removed his tunic and stepped in. He immediately sank to his waist.

Cold as a musk ox's behind!

The bottom was muddy. Methodically, he explored each section with his feet. When that yielded nothing, he held his breath and let his body sink under, feeling through the muck with his hands. He succeeded only in making the water murkier. After several minutes, he concluded that nothing as large as the missing Blade could possibly be there. He climbed out, shivering, and got dressed. To warm up, he ran part of the way to the next spring. He arrived before the Sun reached its zenith.

At Moon Spring, too, Sev searched the banks but found no indication of any recent disturbance. He made another offering and carried out another careful search of the waters. All he got for his efforts were muddy hands and a deepening chill.

Maybe I'm wrong about what they were saying. I'm pretty sure I heard 'blade', but maybe they weren't talking about the Blade of Eagles. Maybe they didn't say 'spring'. It could have been 'string', or 'ring'. Or maybe I'm right, but the spirits didn't accept my offerings. I should have used something better than small starstones. But I can't give up the search now.

He continued on to Whispering Spring, the last in the band's range that he could reach before it got late. Here, the ground was sandier. It was easy to see that no one had been digging around the edges of the spring. Sev reached into the

water up to his elbow. The sediment at the bottom of the spring felt gritty. He cut off a piece of his tunic and offered it together with his last starstone.

"Hey-o. Spirits of these waters, guardians of the secrets of the deep earth. I am Sev, son of Ené. I desperately need your help to recover a special blade of my father's that has been taken, I think, to your realms. Please accept all that I can offer and help me find what has been lost. Hey-o."

Then he stripped once again and stepped in, almost to his navel.

After yet another systematic exploration of the bottom yielded nothing, Sev turned to wade out, despondent. Just then, his foot slid across something sharp. He gingerly traced the hard edge with his toes. Was it just a rock?

He sucked in his breath and plunged down.

The stone was fairly easy to remove from its shallow cover of sand. When he brought it up to the surface and wiped the water from his eyes, he was looking at the Blade of Eagles.

It was twice the length of his hand. Sev couldn't believe how thin it was. How could all those flakes have been removed so precisely from one pointed end to the other without breaking the grey thunderstone? Only a master could have made it, and it was worth a small fortune in furs and beaded buckskin. Its leather grip was undamaged. Sev felt as though he could jump right out of the spring and land standing on the bank. He gently placed the blade on the bank and climbed out of the water. After pulling his tunic on, he gathered several bunches of long grass to pad the Blade in his bag. Then he headed back to camp — straight for his father's tent.

Ené was incredulous, almost giddy.

"Son, you amaze me! Even before undergoing your initiation, you've truly earned a place in the Lion Lodge!" He executed a few excited but cramped dance steps in the tent.

"Oh, Father, and father of my father, shades of the past, shades of the present. I thank you for your guidance of my son, Sev. I thank you for the recovery of the Blade of Eagles. I thank you for your help in our endeavours. Please continue to keep us under your protection so that your descendants may live and prosper. I thank you."

Together, Sev and his father dug a pit under Ené's sleeping mat. They carefully laid the Blade in the bottom, surrounded it with the grass padding, and then filled the pit back up with the dirt they had removed. Ené replaced his sleeping mats and pelts and patted them down.

"Don't forget, Sev, you must not tell anyone we've found the Blade. We'll give the Lodge members a surprise!"

Sev returned to his tent well after dusk, his spirits soaring above the trees toward the stars.

CHAPTER FIFTEEN

A BID FOR INITIATION

There was a lot left to do before the next full Moon. Ené sent Sev to a number of families in the Wolf and Antelope Clans up and downriver, including his sister's family. He'd entrusted Sev with message sticks, notched to indicate the amount of loans that needed to be repaid, or requests for new loans to be made.

Ené himself spent much of his time with families within the Fording encampment, trying to borrow the last items needed for the initiation payment, especially fine buckskin for tunics, fur caps and fur pelts. Yana and Asha busied themselves making sure that all their finest clothes were cleaned and in good repair, sewing on a few more shell beads as they could get them. They used every spare moment to make new buckskin shirts or fur caps, even working at night beside grease lamps. They cleaned all around the tent, ensured there was abundant firewood and washed all their finest mats. They went to the collecting fields to dig lily roots, visited the marshy areas along streams to dig cattail roots and used hooked sticks to strip any remaining hazelnuts from trees.

Kiré spent the last days before the feast hunting and managed to bring back a buck.

Meanwhile, Sev redoubled his efforts to snare white hares. He also tried to meet with Lorea, but she was being closely supervised and all his attempts fell into water.

Finally, the day came. Sev was recruited to help his mother with the final preparations. There were special boiling stones to be collected for heating soup in the bark buckets and the remaining blackberries to be gleaned from thickets around the river. There were grease bones to be broken open, marrow to be extracted, and then the bones needed to be smashed into small pieces so that the remaining fats could be boiled out of them. Sev brought yet more firewood and fresh, clear water from Ferret Creek. He brought armloads of sweet-smelling juniper and fir boughs to strew on the ground where the guests would sit.

As the Sun entered its third quarter, he couldn't stop fidgeting with the fringes of his tunic, and he couldn't keep his eyes from where the path disappeared into the trees. He stared as if he could summon movement with his gaze alone.

"Mother, when will the men arrive? Everything's been ready since midday." His mother was dressed in her finest buckskin tunic and had rubbed fir boughs over her arms and neck to create pleasant smells.

"Don't concern yourself, son. They'll come. Important people like to take their time."

Sev scanned the path yet again. Finally, he was relieved to see a procession of seven eagle plumes advancing from the bushes. Sev thought that they looked rather odd, but he reminded himself that only the highest-ranking members of the Lodge wore plumes.

They must be important.

Bits of white eagle down became detached from the headpieces and floated along with the procession as they approached, as they were intended to. The Lodge members arrived attired in rich, fringed tunics with lines of small red triangles and dots painted in striking patterns. Each also wore a headpiece fashioned with hawk or eagle feathers, and around their necks or wrists were dibat strings of tusk shells and other shell beads from distant waters. Benat, the Headman, was leading. He carried three long darts laid across his arm, along with an antler spearthrower whose end was shaped like an antelope with its rump and tail in the air as the hook.

Sev's father, Leopard's Paw, was clothed in finely curried buckskin, with fringes along the sleeves and white shell beads sewn in stunning lines. Above his ear, he stroked his white fox fur hat as he cordially greeted all seven members, including Raven's Eye. In the area they had cleared in front of the tent, he invited them to sit on woven rush mats laid over fir boughs around the fire. The three highest-ranking members seated themselves cross-legged on the right side of the fire, the others on the left. Opposite the tent, at the head of the hearth between the two groups, lay the three piles of assembled gifts, covered by reindeer skins.

Passing around a bark bowl of cool water, Leopard's Paw announced that he was honoured by his guests' presence at this great event. As was the custom, he again welcomed each member by name, title and rank. He beseeched the great Lion Spirit to look favourably upon those assembled.

Sev stayed in the tent, out of view, but peeked out through a gap in the tent flap. He recognized Benat, Izar, Raven's Eye and Yurok. The other two men seemed to be from elsewhere.

"As you know," Leopard's Paw continued, "we have worked under some duress to meet our obligations to the Lion Lodge so that my son, Sev, can be considered for training and membership. I know that you won't be disappointed with him. Sev is hard-working and intelligent. He may not always be prudent, but he is still young. He has many talents and he respects the spirits. In consideration of our request, please enjoy these foods that we have prepared especially for you."

Yana, Osane and Asha, all dressed in fringed white buckskin decorated with red and yellow ochre patterns, came out carrying bark buckets of hot bone-grease soup, freshly roasted deer ribs, newly preserved kurkan strips that smelled of heady smoked meat, cattail roots, buckets of blackberries, lily roots and buckets of shelled hazelnuts. The guests appeared solemn as they were served some of each dish in their wooden bowls. Leopard's Paw remained standing and did not partake in their feasting.

After all were sated, Izar rose to address the gathering.

"Brother Lions, we have come today to accept a youth for training into our Lodge. He has much promise. I predict a great future for him. However, he must not expect it to come without difficulty. Indeed, we must all suffer to learn the secrets of life and the Lodge."

He continued on, extolling the many benefits and values and virtues of the Lion Lodge. Finally, he acknowledged the feast that had been prepared.

Sev sighed. *At last, he's finished.*

Turning to Leopard's Paw, Izar concluded, "We invite Leopard's Paw to demonstrate that he has met the requirements for us to proceed."

"I am honoured, esteemed members of the Lodge, that you have chosen my son, Sev, to join you in your important work and that you have agreed to share your deep knowledge of the hidden secrets with him. I would like to give you all a small token of my appreciation." Leopard's Paw then crossed the ground to the first of the covered piles and removed the reindeer skin.

"Noble guests, I offer these gifts in thanks. May they aid you in your duties and bring satisfaction to your meals. Please accept these woven mats, thunderstone cores and bark buckets filled with freshly smoked and dried kurkan."

The men were expressionless. They didn't move.

They're like stones.

Leopard's Paw proceeded to the second pile and removed the hide covering. "These large buckets contain cattail roots, soft buckskin hides, fur caps and white hare pelts. I hope these will provide pleasure and comfort."

"Let us see these caps and hides," Izar ordered.

Leopard's Paw handed him a cap and a folded buckskin hide. The Shaman held it up, felt its softness and brought it to his nose, inhaling deeply. "Well smoked." He examined the cap and then passed both items around to the group.

When the Lodge members had finished examining the cap and buckskin, Sev's father paused in silence, as if he were carrying a great weight. Then he walked to the third heap.

He paused again. "Now, I present to you my most honourable possessions, so that you may all benefit from this new initiation." He flung off the cover.

The Lodge members stared past the buckets of food, past the caps and furs piled high, past the fringed buckskin shirts and the strings of shell and ivory beads strewn at the base of the third pile. Their eyes were fixed on the wolf's head and its splendid pelt spread atop the mound. In the wolf's open mouth rested the Blade of Eagles.

There was an astounded silence. Sev craned his neck to see Raven's Eye, who stared as though invisible talons were prying his eyes wide.

All at once, he seemed to choke. Izar stood and abruptly thanked Leopard's Paw. He announced that Sev's training would begin at the next full Moon.

Unceremoniously, the other guests rose. They each took a hefty portion of the gifts, placing them in net bags to take away. Benat took the Blade of Eagles and the wolf pelt. They left the thunderstone cores and rabbit skins.

THE EYES OF THE LEOPARD

CHAPTER SIXTEEN

MEETING IN THE SHADOWS

Since the great migration hunt, the meat from the slaughter had been dried and packed away in raised caches to keep as food for the cold season and as trading reserves. After conferring with the family heads, Benat announced that there would be a communal hunt for any of the reindeer that had remained in the sheltered forests of the valley to spend the cold season. Fresh meat meant that the kurkan reserves could be kept for periods of poor hunting and for trade and was always more than welcome in the Moons leading up to cold season's arrival. Only the best hunters and a few dispatchers would bring down the animals, but many others would be needed to serve as drivers and to set and attend the nets that would stretch from the river to the base of the cliffs.

The morning of the hunt, Sev went to retrieve his father's net from the family cache. Climbing the notched log to the elevated platform, he entered the roughly made structure of poles and bark slabs. Piles of hide-wrapped kurkan suffused the dim space with a heady aroma. Searching through the many bundles, he located the net and hurried down with it to the meadow.

Finding a space among the line of nets being unrolled, he set his net down. As he began unrolling it, he saw that one of the diamonds had a broken string. Unrolling it further, he saw that there was another, and another, an entire swath of broken strings that rendered his net useless. Had a rat gotten into the cache? What else could have caused such damage?

As he stared at the gaping hole, Bakar and Kip strode by and sniggered.

"That net's as useless as you are! Looks like a whole herd of mammoths could pass through it!"

Sev turned his back, bundled up the ruined net and slunk away. Back inside the cache, he carefully inspected the space for evidence of rodents.

What if all our supplies have been spoiled?

But there were no droppings or urine stains or other shredded material. Everything was intact.

Baffled, he returned with the net to the unmatched men's tent. Men and boys rushed past in the opposite direction, spears or nets in their hands.

He flung his own to the ground and examined it again.

A human rat, more likely. Animals gnaw here and there, in an irregular pattern. This hole is far too neat, as though slashed by a blade, although maybe a dull blade. The damaged fibres look coarsely cut, not ragged as if gnawed. The only thing that can cut like this is the edge of a stone flake. This must be Bakar's work — or at least his idea. Those stinking hyenas!

Then Sev remembered that the roll of bramble cordage that he'd collected for his mother was still wedged in the edge of the tent. With all the events and preparations for the Lodge feast, he had forgotten to give it to her. Taking several lengths, he looped the narrowest inner bark strips through the diamond-shaped openings above and below the gash and tied them. He tugged; it held. Satisfied with the repair, he rolled up the net.

Not the best looking, but it will hold, I'm sure.

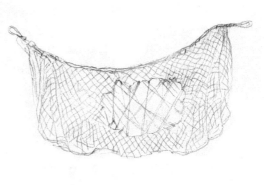

By the time he got to the edge of the woods, the only place left to set up was at the very end of the line, near the valley wall.

This isn't the most prominent position, but at least I'm part of the drive. If Bakar's plan had succeeded, I'd have missed all the excitement. And people would have noticed that I wasn't helping. I can't afford that, not before my initiation.

Next to him, Urtzi was second to last in the line. Although he was too old to hunt, his eyes and ears were still keen.

"Is it too late to join my net to yours?" Sev asked.

"We have time," Urtzi replied. "The women and children are still taking their places, up the valley. Pretty soon, they'll start yelling and beating drums to frighten the deer into our line of nets."

He eyed Sev's net. "I see yours has been badly damaged. A deer could easily break through that clumsy repair. I'll stake it at the very end where nothing's likely to come and I can monitor it from my own net. Here, take my spear and go tell Ekain I said you should help the dispatchers. Hurry!"

Sev grinned.

"Go!"

Sev scanned the expanse of meadow for Ekain. He spotted the antlers of his headdress quickly and ran to them.

Ekain looked Sev up and down. "You dispatched a reindeer during the big migration hunt, didn't you?"

Sev nodded.

"Was that your first reindeer kill?"

Sev nodded again.

"Let's see if you can do it this time too. You can be a dispatcher for your uncle. He's set up at a blind in the trees, just behind the third net. See it? And remember to watch out for the hind legs."

When Sev arrived at Kiré's blind, he found his uncle crouched with Aros's brother, Eneko, behind a thin wall of stout branches stuck in the ground.

"Any animals between the drivers and the nets will have to come near one of our blinds," Kiré whispered. "If I hit one and it goes to the left, Eneko, you track it down. If it goes to the right, Sev, you follow it. Let's hope for two or three fat bucks."

They fell silent as the drivers' distant, shrill shouts and clacking of sticks began to descend into the valley. Sev watched his uncle place a long dart on the hook at the end of his spearthrower. He stood poised with his throwing arm tensed, watching.

Long moments passed at the blind, the drivers' yells and beats coming closer still. Then an antlered head poked through the bushes before them. Kiré waited as the animal strutted past, only ten paces away. When it turned its head, ears twitching, he rose.

Startled, the bull jumped. The spear hit its hind quarter, and it hobbled away, weapon still embedded in its thigh. Eneko took off like a hare. Both disappeared into the bushes.

"Bad aim," Kiré muttered. He squatted back down behind the blind. After a time, the drivers came into sight.

"It looks like there won't be any more today, Sev," his uncle sighed. "Maybe the other hunters had better luck. Let's go to see if Eneko brought down that bull. Don't worry. With the reindeer you brought in at the migration hunt, I expect you'll soon be a full-fledged hunter."

In total, two reindeer and a prized red deer had been caught in the sweep of the valley, one of which entangled itself in the nets. It was enough fresh meat for days, as well as a small community feast.

Sev stayed around the main campfire late that night, listening to Izar's celebratory beating of the hoop drum. He saw Lorea sitting among the women and girls on the opposite side of the fire.

As the drumbeats ended, the Shaman commanded, "Draw near. Open your ears. I will tell you the sacred tale of the Bear Woman, our ancestress.

"Before men lived here, animals roamed the earth. Mammoths, aurochs, bison, deer, reindeer, hyenas, leopards, cave lions and bears. The all-powerful Sky People looked down through the hole in the sky, the Centre Star. They saw the abundant game here and hungered for the taste of meat. They imagined the rich grease in their mouths. Zerua was the first to be brave enough to descend from the Sky World to feast on this abundance.

"Zerua was a powerful Shaman. He entered his sky-tent and began to chant. Soon the tent started to shake and a light — like the blue fire of the Centre Star — appeared in the centre of the floor. Zerua stepped into that light and sank through it, deeper and deeper. He floated down, like the down of an eagle, drifting gently through the sky to the earth. At last, his feet touched the ground, right up there in Bottom-in-the-Air Meadow. He saw a field of strawberries that spread out all around him like red stars in a sky of green. He found them delicious and ate and ate his fill. But the strawberries had a strange effect upon him. He began to burp and belch. He passed gas from both ends!

"The loud noises alerted a young female bear that had come to the meadow looking for strawberries. She wondered if the strange noises were made by a male bear, trying to lure her with mating calls. She stood up and saw, from a distance, a creature unlike any she had ever seen before. This made her more curious, and she came closer.

"Zerua caught her powerful fetor and watched as she approached, walking on two legs. He liked her smell and imagined what she must look like without her fur. As he had no wife in this new world, he decided to use his powers to change this bear into a companion. He greeted her with kind words. Then he took a potent powder from his pouch and threw it over her. As he did so, he recited an incantation to change her into a more comely form. Before his eyes, the bear bent down and removed her fur cloak and her bear mask. When she rose, transformed, he admired her enticing beauty. She admired him as well. They embraced."

The older boys around the fire broke into giggles. Some of the older men grinned. Izar waved his arm for them to be quiet.

"In time, Zerua taught the bear to speak. She taught him how to catch fish. Together, they had many children. Those children became your grandfathers and the grandfathers before them. And so it was. And so it is."

Izar beat a strong rhythm on his drum. The women around the fire broke into the Bear Song, their voices ascending with the sparks, rising above the trees to reach the realm of the Sky ancestors.

Why were the older boys laughing? I don't understand what's so funny, except for the farting. I wonder what Lorea thinks of it. But apparently I can't be friends with her or talk to her anymore now that she's promised to Bakar.

His gaze wandered over to the other side of the fire, just in time to see Lorea get up and disappear behind into the dark.

He rose and stepped away from the firelight. Enveloped by shadows, he made his way over to the tangle of undergrowth behind the women's side.

I don't have a chance anymore, so why am I even bothering? But she seemed to like me, too. Maybe it's true she doesn't want to marry Bakar. I just need to know.

A crackle of twigs made him start. He could see a dim form on the path. He held his breath.

If it's not Lorea, I'll have to explain what I'm doing lurking behind the women's area. He wiped sweaty palms on his tunic.

The figure came closer.

"Is that you, Sev?"

"Yes. You have good night vision!" He coughed. "I saw you go into the bush, and I wanted to talk to you. I heard you've been promised to Bakar."

She didn't reply, but he saw the dark forms of her arms as she crossed them over her chest.

"Is that your choice?" Sev continued.

"What do *you* think? Come. Let's move farther away from the fire, where no one can hear."

They took a few steps off the path, then ducked into the centre of a small grove of alders.

"Don't you know? It was my *father's* decision. I had a big quarrel with him over it. But he's stubborn and sees all kinds of advantages to the match. My opinions don't count for much. Bakar's family has wealth and standing. There's nothing I can do about it, unless I run away. And where would I go? They'd only find me. I can't fend for myself all alone."

"I'm glad you don't want to be with Bakar."

"I don't even like him! He thinks too much of himself, and he's nasty. But I don't have a choice. My father is taking me back to the Pine Barrens tomorrow. I was hoping to see you before I left. I have something for you. Here."

Sev held out his hand. Lorea placed a smooth object in his palm, about the size of a grouse egg. She folded his fingers over it, holding them for a moment before letting go.

"What is it?"

"Can you guess?"

"It feels polished, but lighter and warmer than a stone."

"It's a visionstone. My father told me that it was washed onto a shore far away in the north. You can wear it or carry it as a talisman. They say it has magical and medicinal powers to protect you — and energy that can heal. Maybe you can't see it very well at night, but it's yellow and clear, like a drop of the Sun."

Sev tried to study his gift in the darkness.

"When you hold it up in the light, you can sometimes see things in it," Lorea continued.

"Will I see *you* in it?"

"I don't know. You can try."

They both laughed softly.

"It'll pick up little things when you rub it on your tunic, and it'll burn too. So be careful. Smells like tree sap when it burns." Lorea hesitated. "Maybe it'll protect you during your initiation trials. I've heard awful stories."

"So have I. I'll just have to do the best I can." He looked toward the distant firelight. "Do you think spirits can control what happens?"

"I don't know. I see your Shaman wears a visionstone-bead necklace, so it must have some kind of power. Maybe it helps him contact the spirits or get their blessings. Now you have a visionstone too." She hesitated. "Sometimes, things I hope for do happen, as if a spirit listened to my thoughts. Or maybe whispered what to do in my ear. I do think that there are powers we can't see."

"No spirits ever whispered in my ear. But sometimes I make offerings to ask for their help — just in case they really are around. Maybe a spirit will whisper something in your ear about *me!*"

Lorea didn't reply. It was impossible to see her expression in the darkness. Softly, she stepped forward. Her forehead touched his.

The hairs on the back of his neck rose and cold water ran down his spine. They stood together like that for what seemed like a long moment.

"I have to go now. Please take care of yourself," Lorea said.

"I will, don't worry. You take care of yourself, too. I don't think Bakar has very good intentions for you."

He waited some time after she had gone before leaving the grove.

Back by the fire, he turned the visionstone over and over in his hand. It felt warm. He held it up to his eye and could see distorted flames flickering through the clear amber. He thought he could see a vague form in its depths, too, like a person.

CHAPTER SEVENTEEN

ORDEAL

As the new Fox Moon showed its thin crescent following the communal hunt it became noticeably colder, though no frost had yet appeared. Sev settled into a routine of target practice, trap setting and making spears, cordage and traps. He tried to be out in the bush whenever he expected Bakar to be around the tent. The work lulled him. It felt as though his life could just continue on like this, adapting only to the slow changes in the seasons and the gradual strengthening of his body.

Trees must experience something like this — just stretching higher as the world changes around them.

Aros returned from visiting his father's sister. As soon as they had a moment alone, Aros dragged Sev into the boys' and unmatched men's tent, peering out through the flap to make sure no one was approaching.

"Sev! I heard that you and Bakar were chosen to be initiated into the Lion Lodge. Is it true?"

"That's what Izar, or the spirits, said from inside his shaking tent. I guess it's an honour, but people say that you can die in the initiation. I'm afraid it might all just be a way of getting rid of me — and maybe my father, too, especially since Bakar is involved. In any case, the feast for the initiation has been given and everything's been paid for. It's settled. But what did you hear?"

"Just that you'd been chosen. People don't talk about the Lion Lodge much, let alone their plans. There can be consequences. I told you not to go into the cave. You don't have much choice, now. You're in the coals, for better or worse. Just be very careful; never let your guard down."

"Yeah, you were right. I guess I was just trying to convince you and Runt that I was worth being friends with."

"Don't worry about that," Aros replied. "We are friends. We shared our blood. We'll stand by you."

"Thanks," Sev said. "That means a lot. I've tried to make up with Runt. I gave him a pecking when I thought he'd told Bakar about the cave. But we went out together to pick up some hares I trapped. He used them to repair his old tunic — I think he's forgiven me."

"Runt may be bold and blabby, but he doesn't go back on his word. He has a good soul. How do you feel about getting into the Lodge?"

"Well, like I said, I don't really know what to think, whether it really is an honour or whether it's all just a way to get rid of me. I sure don't sleep too well thinking about it, especially with Bakar in the same tent. No one has said anything about any initiation since we gave the feast. Maybe they won't do it until the springing-up season. That would be fine by me. I'm not eager to go through any ordeals. I'd really like to move to the tent with Runt, especially if you came along. I've asked a couple of times about it, but they say there just isn't any more space. Hopefully, someday there will be."

◇ ◇ ◇

As the Fox Moon waxed nearly full, Sev focused on a few simple, satisfying tasks: collecting thunderstone cores for the cold season, knapping spear points, tracking and making long darts. The activity occupied his attention, leaving little room for worries. No one said anything more to him about the cave, Xabi or the initiation. For the first time in several Moons, life felt almost normal.

Then, one evening, his calm was shattered. As he sat alone at the tent braiding some cordage, two men with blackened faces and lion's paws hanging from their sleeves appeared out of the woods. They stood in front of him for a moment. Sev didn't know what to say or do. Were they men from the Lodge? Or marauding raiders from the mountains? Then, without uttering a word, they both stepped forward and roughly grabbed his arms, binding them with rawhide rope.

"Hey! Let me go! Let me go!"

Sev struggled to break free, but to no effect. A buckskin hood was pulled over his head. Large hands hoisted him up. The breath was thrust from his lungs as he was thrown onto his abductor's shoulder, the flakes in his waist pouch clinking together. Then they were moving.

It was a long, jostled trek before he was finally set down. When the hood was pulled off and he was unbound, he found himself under an unfamiliar limestone overhang.

"Stay in view of this shelter. Wait. Look for your spirit helper. No drinking. No eating. Three days."

The men left.

Sev huddled against the stone wall, cold and alone. For a long while, he just waited.

Is something going to happen? What am I supposed to do to look for a spirit helper?

But dusk began to darken the colours of the day, and no one else appeared. Finally, he stood and searched the bushes near the shelter for something to make an impromptu fire drill. Although the branches he found were mostly twisted and insubstantial, he managed to find a fairly straight piece for a rod and a larger one for a base. He resharpened some old flakes left in the rock shelter to shape the branches into a useable drill and, with a bit of effort, soon had a small set of flames licking the air.

Squatting beside the fire, he examined the shelter more closely. The back wall displayed several handprints of ground charcoal that had probably been mixed with spit. There were also crude engravings and charcoal sketches of a reindeer, an aurochs, two horses and the hump of a mammoth.

Looks like others have been trying to contact their spirit helpers. Maybe these are the animals they saw in their visions. Or maybe they drew images of the animals to try to summon them as protectors. I should try that. Maybe tomorrow.

From his shelter, he could see Ila, the Moon, coming up over the valley cliffs in her full bright form.

Two more days of this. No signs of any spirit guides at all. Maybe if I just stay still and wait they'll come? An offering might help . . . but what? I can't give Lorea's vision-stone away.

I never even dream about spirits or any powerful animals. Maybe I wasn't born to see them. Maybe I'm too concerned about the practical things. Maybe they don't really exist and dreams are just dreams. But I might as well try. I don't have anything else to do.

There goes my stomach, complaining. Still, it's not as bad as the hunger pains were during the famine.

His thoughts drifted.

I wonder what would have happened if we'd stayed in our home territory. Would I have survived the famine, or would more of us have died? My father was starting to become important there. Maybe he would have been a Headman by now.

Sev absently studied the old, discarded stone flakes and charcoal near his toes. His gaze rested on the embers that remained of his own fire, and he reached for a somewhat dry branch, cut off some shavings and stirred up the coals. Even in the moonlight, he didn't dare go out of sight of the rock shelter to gather more firewood.

He held his hands as close as he could to the small flames, which warmed and entranced him for a while.

Maybe there are spirit images in the flames, if only I could recognize them.

He reached into his pouch and pulled out the visionstone that Lorea had given him. He raised it to his eye, and the fire made dazzling patterns in the stone but nothing that made any sense to him.

Just pretty flickers and flashes.

As the flames died down, he curled up tightly in his tunic and fell asleep.

The next day, he again explored the area just in front of the rock shelter, looking for any signs of a power animal he might be able to contact. At the bottom of the slope leading up to the overhang, the willows and blackberry bushes became dense, and he couldn't go very far into them without losing sight of the shelter. There were no animal droppings or tracks anywhere that he could find. Lying on his back outside the shelter, he tried to envision different shapes in the clouds and the rock face, but nothing convincing appeared. He tried to make an offering of some fringes off of his tunic, but nothing happened. The fasting was only giving him stomach cramps. Staying still for too long made him restless and twitchy.

Giving up on contacting a guardian spirit, Sev contented himself with searching for flakes of thunderstone among the debris left by the previous initiates. Sharpening one of them, he used it to carve a rough figure of a wolf into a stick, but the result hardly looked like an animal of any kind, just some misshapen lumps. Abandoning it, he drew a crude reindeer on his tunic with a piece of charcoal.

He again pulled out the visionstone.

Lorea said it looks like a drop of sunlight. I think it sort of looks like the eye of a leopard, like the one I saw in front of the cave. I'm glad she wanted to give me something to remember her. But what's the point, if she's going to marry Bakar?

Sev was beginning to feel a little light-headed. Trying to distract himself from thinking about Lorea, he began to study the ants and other insects crawling and flying around him. There seemed to be more of them than he'd ever noticed before, and he found himself entranced by their movements and glossy bodies.

Toward dusk, Sev heard a loud rustling in the bushes near the rock overhang. He tensed and waited. After a long silence, there came a guttural, bear-like grunt. It came again, and again, growing steadily louder. Sev flattened himself against the rock wall. His nostrils flared at the sudden, unmistakable fetor of bear feces. He could feel the veins in his head pulsing.

Can this be a test by the Lion Lodge? Or maybe I'm about to meet a power animal. How am I supposed to communicate with it? What if it kills me instead? Am I imagining things, after fasting so long? No. I can hear it and smell it. It's real!

Is completing my initiation worth dying for?

The bushes moved. A barrage of dirt, sticks and stones flew out and struck Sev's arm and head, then a mass of bear feces landed not far from his feet.

What in the stars . . .?

He had to get away. As he jolted away from the overhang onto the path down the slope, the threatening growl was cut short by a cough. A human cough.

Sev stopped and turned.

Tentatively, he approached the bushes. In the failing light, he couldn't make out anything recognizable. There was another growl, followed by movement in the branches, then a thud and a whimper of pain. Mystified, but feeling a stir of anger, Sev plunged into the brush.

This can't be a Lion Lodge Elder, coughing and whining in pain.

He ducked under a low-hanging willow bough.

There on the ground, clutching his ankle, was Bakar. Beside him was a bark tray, bear feces smeared in the bottom. The other boy looked up at him, expression defiant.

"What the wolf's piss do you think you're doing?" Sev demanded.

"What do you *think*, you little nit? Scared you, didn't I?" Bakar struggled into a crouch.

"Snake! You don't deserve to be part of any lodge!"

"*You're* the one who shouldn't be here! You're nobody from nowhere! Anyway, you'll never make it."

"What's *wrong* with you, Bakar? You hide behind your father's name, and you torment everyone who you think might be better than you."

"You killed my best friend!"

"You know that's a lie! I did everything I could to save Xabi. He died because he did something stupid."

"*You* put a spell on him!"

"Ha! If I really *had* any magical powers, I'd have used them to get rid of you, you stinking maggot!"

"As if you could. We'll see who survives the ordeals."

Bakar rose awkwardly to his feet, spat, then hobbled off into the gathering darkness.

"You better not try any more stunts, Bakar!" Sev shouted at his back. "You've already broken the rule of seclusion. Lorea deserves a lot better than *you*, you scum!"

Sev returned to the overhang. It took a while for his rage to subside. He scooped up the bear dung with a piece of bark from around the shelter and threw it into the bush with all his might.

This is a bad state to be in. I need to be calm and clear-headed, in case a spirit helper does try to make contact with me. Maybe that's what Bakar was trying to do — destroy my ability to attract a spirit helper. Or unnerve me so I'd give up before completing the trials. I can't let my anger swallow me. It'll distract me from what I need to do.

Although he was tired and weak from hunger, not even an uneasy sleep came until far into the night.

By the following morning, his hunger pangs had subsided, leaving a hollow, light feeling in his stomach.

No food and no water. Nobody to talk to except the birds, insects and spirits — if there are any out there. What if I get hurt, or a wild animal attacks me and I'm too weak to escape or fight it off? Who would even know what happened to me?

Rain and sleet fell steadily during the day. At one point, Sev noticed a man watching him from a distance down the trail before he continued on.

I guess the Lion Lodge is checking to make sure I'm alive. At least the overhang is dry — as long as the wind doesn't blow too hard.

He carved a few small bits of antler with the stone flake but didn't have the energy to finish anything. He tried to think about power animals, in the hope of summoning them as allies. None appeared. No lions. No aurochs. No mammoths. No bison. No rhinoceroses. No leopards. No bears. Nothing.

Maybe I'm not strong enough to draw the attention of a powerful spirit ally. He passed his fingers through his hair, checking for lice. He crushed the few that he found between his teeth and swallowed them.

His thoughts wandered again to the long journey that had brought his family to the Bears' lands. He didn't remember having to deal with any special lodges where they lived in the Clear Mountains, or during their flight and brief stays with other groups along the way. Maybe they were there but not so powerful, or just not so evident.

Gazing out from the cave, he could just see a strip of sky through a gap in the trees. The rain had lifted, the clouds began to break up. There was a humped cloud that looked like the top of a mammoth seen from behind. There was a craggy one that resembled the open mouth of a lion with a pair of giant teeth. Another appeared like a couple of entwined ferrets, playing or fighting for food.

Are these the visions I'm supposed to have? It doesn't seem right — I'm just inventing them. A real vision should come on its own and be intense, unmistakable.

Dozing throughout the afternoon, Sev found himself half-awake as night descended once again. He spotted the Centre Star between the clouds and imagined himself flying up until he climbed right through that hole of light into the Sky World.

Izar is always talking about animal spirits in the Sky World that are supposed to look like stars. There are two stars shining outside the cave right now. But shouldn't they be higher up? No. They're too big and too close to be stars. They sort of look like a pair of bright yellow eyes, staring at me. Could it be an animal? An owl? Maybe a leopard? It's hard to tell in the dark from this distance. It doesn't blink.

It doesn't approach, either — so maybe it's not an animal. It just seems to be watching. Maybe it's a real spirit helper! Maybe. I wonder if it wants something from me? I wish I wasn't so tired.

He rubbed his eyes and fought to keep them open, but he was too weak with hunger.

Sev drifted back to consciousness in the misty dawn, as the watcher he'd seen earlier appeared on the trail and whistled sharply.

Sev stumbled to his feet, bleary-eyed, and met the man at the bottom of the rock shelter. Without a word, he threw a fur over Sev's back and gestured for Sev to follow.

On the way back to the main encampment, they collected four other initiates. *They must have also been fasting.*

Sev remembered having seen the slightly older novices among the traders and visitors from the Antelope and Wolf Clans who'd come for the big migration hunt.

When they stopped for Bakar, Sev was careful not to look too obviously in his direction, but he glimpsed a slight limp in the other boy's gait as they proceeded.

They were brought to a secluded clearing and instructed to stand behind an imposing man whom Sev didn't recognize. He wore eagle wings on his shoulders, and eagle talons hung down from his beaded headdress. He nodded to them once, solemnly.

"Look only at the ground. Nowhere else. No person. No sound," he commanded. Then he led them from the clearing.

It seemed the entire Bear Clan and every guest stood waiting for them as they went by the camp, lining each side of the path. The Eagle Man led the six youths slowly past the crowd, who wailed and sobbed as if the boys were about to die.

Despite having been ordered not to speak to or look at anyone, Sev stole a sideways glance, hoping to pick out his parents, but his furtive peek was too short to identify anyone.

They continued on to a grove at the other end of the encampment. Two guardians dressed in cloaks of black raven feathers stood next to a fire at one end of the clearing. There, the initiates were told to stand in a circle. A man approached each of them in turn and smeared their faces black with a mixture of powdered charcoal and grease. A harsh voice then commanded the boys to lie face-down on the ground.

Three hoop drums throbbed with a fast, steady beat. There was a sharp crackle above his head, and the image of glowing yellow eyes flashed through Sev's mind as he felt a blaze of heat on his back. He smelled the acrid sweetness of burning pine. A few embers landed on his neck, adding the stink of burning hair. He didn't dare brush them off. Then the flaming branch came down.

Whoosh! Whoosh! Whoosh! The burning bough struck the ground again and again, terrifyingly close to his head.

"Don't look! Eyes closed!" rasped the hard voice.

The drumming continued. The same, loud, insistent beat, over and over. The pounding rhythm began to feel like it was inside Sev's head, echoing in his skull.

One of the novices to his left was directed to stand. A chant arose. "Waaay. Waaay. Waaay." Then, after a long pause, another boy was called. Sev kept his eyes tightly shut and waited.

In a few moments, he felt hands on his arms, forcing him to rise. He was placed in the middle of a large elk hide that had been laid out on the ground and forced to lie down again. Men seized each of its corners and tossed him high into the air, heaving and catching him in the hide several times to the monotone chant.

"Waaay. Waaay. Waaay."

The sky and earth turned over and over. When he was finally returned to his feet, Sev was unable to stand. He fell to his knees.

"Eyes down!"

He felt woozy and sick but tried to focus on the still-turning ground.

Maybe this was how the masked men fell from the sky during Izar's night performance. Maybe they were tossed from a hide into the air and landed in the fire.

Without warning, someone grabbed his hair and began shearing it with a sharp stone blade. More than once, the blade carelessly sliced into his scalp. Sev flinched. In a few moments, most of his hair lay on the ground. While the other initiates' hair was cut he was left waiting, exposed.

"Eyes on the ground!"

The drumming never stopped.

The man with eagle wings addressed the boys in a deep, sonorous tone.

"Novices, take heed! You are about to enter into the spirit world, to embark on a journey that you may not complete. You have come far already, but we cannot promise that you will return to your camps. Some boys stay in the domain of the spirits, in the Sky World. You are about to be eaten by the Mother Lion. If you merit it, the power and magic of the Lion Lodge will guide you safely back to this world. You must show us that you are deserving of the power we have to bequeath. If you are not strong enough to use this power properly, it will destroy you. Even with the aid of the spirit guardian you may acquire through your visions, you must work hard to survive this journey. It will be a supreme test of your courage and your strength. If you still aspire to become members of the Lion Lodge, go now into the world of spirit. And be prepared to die!"

CHAPTER EIGHTEEN

SECRETS OF THE CAVE

They were led up the side of the valley above the river. Dazed and weak from the fasting, Sev could barely put one foot in front of the other in the seemingly endless trek. He had stopped wondering what would happen next.

They reached the narrow plateau above the valley and descended the slope on the other side into the ravine of Raven Creek. As they rounded a rock face, he saw a man standing next to a cave, the same sacred cave that he'd entered a few Moons ago. They had come to it by a different path. The surrounding birch trees, now barren, gave the scene a haunted look. Remembering his vow to return, Sev felt a pang of anxiety. He hadn't expected that it would be like this.

"No tunics," announced the guardian at the cavern's entrance. The initiates removed their tunics and stood naked in the cold air.

"Wait here." The guardian disappeared into the cave. The silence outside hung heavily. When he reappeared, the guardian was holding several burning pine sticks. He motioned the youths to follow. They entered the cave in single file. Sev was third in line, behind Bakar.

The pine torches dispelled the cave's gloom. As the group moved deeper inside, the guardian stopped in front of the black handprint and red dots on the wall. The aurochs loomed above. The initiates gazed mutely at the images for several moments before they were motioned on.

A little farther in, a tall slab of stone hung down from the ceiling, like a cascade of water frozen in its flow. Sev couldn't remember seeing it before, but maybe they'd gone down a different passage. He was having trouble focusing.

The guardian struck one of the stone folds three times with his fist. The impact made a booming sound that echoed through the cave. In response, drums began beating a slow rhythm from deep within the darkness.

The procession threaded its way along a different route than Sev had taken, penetrating farther than he had. Entering a narrow passage, the youths stepped into puddles. Clay gushed between Sev's toes.

The guardian swiped his pine torches against the wall. They flared with renewed strength.

"Wraaaak! Aaark!"

A screeching figure sprang out from the shadows. It seemed to be half-human and half-bird — its eyes, nose and mouth were black and sharp. Another shriek came from somewhere behind the boys.

The last boy in line jumped out of reach of the second birdman's sharp talons. The group clustered behind the guardian, who waved his staff as the creatures descended upon them. One birdman managed to scratch the arm of the Antelope Clan initiate before the guardian banished the threatening beings back into a dark alcove.

They walked on, through a slender tunnel that opened into another long chamber. It was a wonder-world of crystal icicles, dripping water that flashed in the torchlight. A world of suspended, flowing stone.

The group stopped to gaze at the bison, mammoths and lions painted on the cavern walls.

"Spirits," was all the guardian said.

The faint drumming became louder as they proceeded into the cavern. It was now mixed with spirit whistles and chanting voices. After traversing another dim passage, the boys finally arrived in a large chamber. A fire of burning bones in the centre illuminated a circle of five costumed men. There was one lion-headed being, plus the ones that he'd seen earlier — the two dressed in raven feathers and the one with eagle feathers, as well as a man covered in bear skin. Sev looked around carefully.

No flying moles.

Despite the disguises, Sev recognized Raven's Eye as one of the feathered men. Standing at the center was Izar with two others beating hoop drums. The sounds echoed into the far recesses of the cave, beyond the light.

Sev had started to sway, mesmerized, when two more beings with lions' heads emerged stealthily from the shadows. Their prowl around the fire turned into a dance of lunging movements followed by vibrating legs and outstretched arms, forcing the initiates to step back as the lions came near. The men in the bird costumes joined in the dance around the fire, swooping to brush some of the boys with their wings as they twirled. Sev winced as some wing feathers streaked across his face.

Another man-lion moved to the front of the fire. The head and skin that he wore almost completely covered his own hair and face, his arms and his back.

That must be Benat.

The wall behind him displayed a central painted lion with other lions and horses around it. The Master Lion raised his staff and brought it down with a thud. Everything stopped except for the intermittent, distant drip of water.

Silence filled the air.

"So! You would be members of the Lion Lodge?"

No one made a sound.

"Speak!"

"Yes," mumbled Sev, with the others.

"You understand that you will begin as members of the lowest rank?"

There was more mumbled assent.

"Rraaaaarggghhh!" The deafening roar resonated throughout the cavern.

"You must demonstrate your worth, your mettle, your respect for our traditions, your willingness to suffer and to follow the path of the Lion wherever it may lead. We hold the powers of life! You must show that you are strong enough and worthy of receiving these powers. You must earn the right to have us share them with you.

"Watch."

At his signal, the other two lion-headed beings leapt forward and attacked one of the drummers. The man screamed and pleaded for his life, but the creatures pulled him down. They tore into his flesh, clawed open his stomach, and pulled out his guts, lapping up blood.

At last, the Master Lion strode in, dealt the two beasts several heavy blows with his staff and pushed them away. They darted into the cave's dark reaches, their mouths dripping red.

The Master Lion knelt over the dead drummer and partially covered him with a hide. He placed the tangled entrails back inside the body and drew the hide up over the ravaged corpse. Then he rose and planted his staff beside the man's head. He intoned a chant whose words Sev did not understand.

With his staff, the Master Lion struck the ground next to the dead man's stomach. Kneeling once again, he made a sharp gesture. Another Lodge member produced a bark bowl of water, which the Master Lion blew into three times. He sipped deeply without swallowing, and sprayed water from his mouth over the dead drummer's stomach and head. He spoke more arcane words over the man.

The man's eyelids fluttered. His lips quivered. The Master Lion lifted the drummer's head and raised the water bowl to his lips. The man drank! Then he propped himself up on an elbow and very slowly staggered to his feet.

Sev's mind reeled.

There must be some explanation.

He scanned the cave floor. Some intestines and a torn, shaven hide protruded from beneath a sprawling buckskin that was spread out behind the place where the man had lain. They were barely visible by the firelight. *Another trick of the Lodge — like the men who fell from the sky.*

Moving to stand in front of the initiates, the Master Lion spoke.

"You are all witnesses. It is we who can ward off enemy spirits and restore the dead to life. We can teach you the secrets of the Sky and the Earth. You can learn to transform yourselves into bears and lions. Acceptance into the Lodge will increase your strength and power and bring you wealth. We can help your families too. But you must prove yourselves worthy, and you must swear never to reveal the secrets of the Lodge. Those who reveal our secrets will die

horrible deaths. They will be eaten alive by lions, never to be brought back."

Peering into the eyes of each initiate in turn, he demanded, "Do you so promise?"

All thoughts fled, as Sev was transfixed by the piercing gaze.

"Yes."

"So be it. Now accept the first mark of the Lodge."

One of the costumed men painted a red line with three dots beneath it across each of Sev's blackened cheeks — then a line down his chin and a pointed shape on his forehead like a downward spearhead. The man held up a dried lion's paw, fitted with small, sharp flakes of sunstone between the claws. He raked them firmly over Sev's upper arm. Three fresh cuts burned fiercely, even after the man washed them with water and rubbed a mixture of grease and charcoal into the incisions.

The other initiates all endured the same procedure. Bakar grimaced and whimpered as blood seeped from his gashes. The costumed man scowled at him.

The Master Lion proclaimed, "Your skin has been torn by the Lion of the Lodge. Soon you will die from your wounds. You must retreat into the dark now — to die alone. Let your former life die. You must seek your spirit ally who will bring you back from death, to guide you to your new life. Open yourself to the spirits and feel the power of this sacred place. Now go!"

One of the guardians lit two pairs of pitch torches and waved Sev to follow him. He led Sev along a narrow corridor, winding even deeper into the earth. Eventually, the man pointed to a recess barely large enough for a person to crouch in and handed Sev one pair of the slim, lit pitch sticks. Without uttering a word, he turned and went back the way he had come, his torchlight dwindling into darkness.

With growing unease, Sev raised his own feeble torch to scan the close walls of the alcove. A number of attempts at animal drawings were scratched in the stone. Many of the marks were little more than scribbles.

What does the Lodge expect me to do?

Spying a stone flake not far from his feet, Sev tried scratching a mammoth on the wall like the one he imagined in the clouds. Before he had finished, the flame of the pitch stick he held in his other hand began to wane. Swiping the torch against the wall didn't help. The flame flickered and died.

He was left in complete blackness, deeper than he'd ever known. The only sounds were those distant drops, falling into puddles somewhere in the dark.

How long do I have to be here? How long can someone survive without food or water? It's already been three days since I've eaten.

The cuts on his arm were still alive with pain.

After endless moments, he started to notice faint flashes in the dark, like dim sparks. They multiplied and danced in patterns, like nets of stars.

This must be a dream — or a vision. But I'm sure I'm awake.

The flashes faded, and a pair of yellow eyes opened and fixed on him. *Those look like the same eyes I saw from the rock shelter. They're watching me.*

Eventually, the eyes dimmed and disappeared, and the flashes returned, though less frequent than before. He realized that he was shivering.

Have I really been left to die? But why? I wish I wasn't here. I wish all of this was over.

He closed his eyes.

The sound of a rock hitting the wall in front of him startled Sev awake. His shoulders ached from his hunched position.

He had no idea how long he'd dozed.

He blinked. A light was approaching through the dark. *Are my eyes tricking me again?*

But the light came steadily closer. It was a torch, held by the same guardian who had escorted him to the alcove. As the man neared, Sev unfolded himself and stiffly rose, but his legs buckled. He grabbed for the rock wall.

I'm like an old man.

The man gestured for Sev to follow. Fighting light-headedness, he walked behind the guardian back to the main chamber. The circle of disguised men still stood around the fire. The other novices were already there.

"Welcome to the Lodge of Light and Life!" intoned the Master Lion. "You have been in darkness. Your former body and name are now dead. You are to forget them. Great Lion Spirit, we beseech you to give these new initiates the water of life. Give them the meat of growth, the grease of abundance, the wisdom of the Lodge. Give them clean, strong bodies. Give them new lives and new names."

A man offered Sev water. He drank deeply. He stood, eyes closed, as he was scrubbed of the smudged charcoal and paint with damp, shredded bark. The cuts on his arm continued to sting. Someone handed Sev a bark bowl of warm, oil-rich soup with reindeer meat. It was the most delicious thing Sev had ever tasted.

The food of the Sky People must taste like this.

The Master Lion placed a fur robe around Sev's shoulders and proclaimed, "Your name is now 'Sun Server', so named after the Follower of the Sun."

He leaned over Bakar with a similar robe.

"Your name is now 'Crossed Viper'."

That suits him.

Sev edged closer to the fire. With the soup and the warmth, a vestige of his strength began to return. After the other four initiates were named, the drumming, whistling, chanting and animal dances resumed.

Finally, the Master Lion raised his staff once more.

"You have all done well. You have earned your entrance into the Lion Lodge. You will learn many things in the coming seasons about the ways of Osti, the Sun, and Ila, the Moon, Father and Mother of the Sky People. You will learn to always honour and preserve our connections to our ancestors in the Sky and on the Earth, for they were and still are powerful beings. The images on these walls are ways to contact them. Their spirits can be found in this cave. There is much that you must be taught as you progress in the Lodge, much to learn, and at considerable cost. But now is a time to celebrate. Return to the world outside, to your families, and prepare to begin your new lives!"

CHAPTER NINETEEN

THE GROOMING

They were led back to the cave's entrance and instructed to discard their fur robes. When they stepped outside, naked, into the light of a full Moon, they were presented with new buckskin pants and fringed shirts. At the touch of the soft, freshly tanned hide, Sev's skin came alive. The rich, smokey smell permeated his head. He saw his old tunic and waist pouch in a pile just outside the entrance and quickly recovered the pouch.

In the sky, the Sun's Follower dutifully preceded Ila, the Moon, and contributed a few rays of light over the entourage as the fatigued youths were marched back over the crest of the ridge, along the narrow plateau and down the slope into the river valley.

Fires glowed at the camp below like stars. Sev felt as if he were flying. He was a long dart, catapulted through the cool air, soaring into the Sky World.

The initiates' arrival was accompanied by loud drumbeats. Everyone crowded around the arrivals, now smiling and laughing. Sev saw his mother and sister standing with Kiré, and he broke away from the group. Kiré gave him a long, tight hug. His mother and sister did the same.

"What was it like, Sev?" demanded Osane.

"You shouldn't call me 'Sev' anymore. My new name is 'Sun Server'. And I'm not allowed to tell you anything about what happened."

"You look funny with your hair all cut off and smudges all over your face."

Kiré interrupted, grinning. "Let's go to our family's tent, Sev — that is, Sun Server. We've got a lot of feasting to do! You must be as hungry as a lion, as you might say now."

At Leopard Paw's tent, they huddled together on mats around the fire outside. With a big smile, Yana placed before them bark buckets filled with freshly roasted meat, fish, nuts and roasted cattail roots. Osane fed scraps of reindeer meat to the two wolf cubs. Her pleading had finally made their father agree to keep the cubs for future needs and to impress others in the meantime. Sev stuffed as much into his mouth as he could but was frustrated to find that his stomach had shrunk during his fast. As he slowly chewed his third cattail root dipped in grease, his father approached, leading three older men in decorated buckskin shirts and fringed pants.

"Sun Server, this is White Bison, Rising Sun and Swift Wing. They are members of the Lion Lodge from the Wolf Clan, our neighbours upriver. I've asked them to join us in our celebration of your achievement. Noble members of the Lodge, please make yourselves comfortable on our fine mats around the fire. Son Sev, or Sun Server, you must know how proud I am! I wish to declare this to everyone here." Sev wondered if any of these men had been cloaked in bird or animal costumes at the initiation.

His father drew from behind him a robe trimmed with fox and lynx fur.

"This is a special lynx robe, made by your mother with furs from the Clear Mountains." He draped the hide over his son's shoulders. "And here is a spearthrower, the Star Striker. It is to be used only on special occasions. It was made by Turq, the master carver. My father gave it to me when I was old enough to marry."

He placed a long piece of antler in Sev's hand. The flickering firelight revealed a bird carved at its end, the beak bent to form a hook for attaching long darts.

Kiré, Yana, Osane, all gasped, eyes wide, and the three visitors congratulated Sev with effusive words, each in turn.

Sev thanked his family sincerely but didn't know what to say to the visitors. *Why did he give me these gifts in front of them?*

"Our guests have eligible daughters," Sev's father continued. "It is time we begin thinking about a wife for you. I know you're still young, but you are now an important member of the Bear Clan, and a good marriage can take many cold seasons of preparation."

"Honoured guests. Tell your clan that my son will be a strong match partner. As an initiate of the Lion Lodge, he has a promising future. He will bring respect and prosperity to the family of any woman he marries. Please accept these small gifts for the trouble you have taken to attend our feast."

Leopard's Paw gave each of the Lodge members a birchbark bucket containing dried kurkan and a well-executed antler engraving of horses. Although the guests maintained a solemn demeanour, they were clearly pleased.

Sev turned away to conceal his dismay. *So, finding me a wife is just another trade deal! Why can't I choose someone for myself? If I can't marry Lorea, maybe I can find someone else like her.*

No, it wouldn't be the same.

His father now was discussing the hunting farther upriver and trade prospects with the Wolf Clan. Sev's thoughts drifted as he stared into the fire. Every muscle in his body ached.

Eventually, the visitors departed. Leopard's Paw drew Sev aside.

"I know you are very tired, son, but before you go to the uplands tomorrow to heal your initiation wounds in isolation, I must tell you this. Though Bakar's family, too, is celebrating tonight, they have suffered a serious setback. Everyone now knows that it was Raven's Eye who arranged the theft of the Blade of Eagles. It seems he hoped to profit by exchanging it with my trading competitors. Clearly, he thought that the Blade would make him wealthy enough to seal a marriage agreement with Lorea's family. He also must have hoped to damage my standing in the clan and my reputation in exchanges. Now that his plans have fallen into water, you must be on your guard. It is better that he does not learn how the Blade was found, or you will be in danger. Raven's Eye has seniority and influence in the Lodge. He is still powerful, and can be vengeful. Let them think that it was the spirits who returned it."

Sev was too exhausted to absorb this new worry. As his father ducked away into the tent, he gazed up at the Moon. The Sun's Follower was descending with it toward the horizon, and he smiled. Wrapped in his warm lynx robe, he rolled the taste of the succulent food on his tongue. His arm still pained him, and it felt like the drums of the cave were still throbbing in his head.

His last thoughts were of Lorea, as his soul drifted gently into dreams like a canoe on placid water — a canoe watched by two yellow eyes.

CHAPTER TWENTY

THE EYES OF THE LEOPARD

A t dawn, Sev was awakened by his father's cry.

"Who's there?"

Two figures, one large and one small, approached cautiously through the morning mists that had invaded the clearing around Ené's tent. As Sev pushed himself upright, Leopard's Paw stepped past him, brandishing a club.

"I am Edur, of the Pine Barrens," came a voice from the taller stranger as they came closer. "This is my daughter, Lorea." He rested his hand on her shoulder. "I would request a word with you, Leopard's Paw."

Sev's father lowered the club.

"Welcome, Edur and Lorea. Please sit." He gestured toward Sev. "This is my son. Last night, he completed his initiation trial with the Lion Lodge. His name is now 'Sun Server'."

Am I dreaming? Sev wondered. *I thought Lorea and her father left days ago.*

Edur nodded to Sev. "We were at the Bear cousins' camp downriver when we heard that it was Raven's Eye who arranged to steal the Blade of Eagles from you. His actions threatened to undermine many important existing trade relations and upset the traditional order in the clan. I had concluded a marriage pact for Lorea with his son, but now such an alliance will only bring shame upon her. We do not want to be associated with a thief, and I feel wary that Bakar may have the same character as his father.

"But I still seek an alliance with a family in one of the Bear clans. Such an alliance would benefit both sides. I would like to discuss an arrangement with you, and I have brought you a gift." He withdrew his hand from under his fur robe and handed Sev's father a gleaming mammoth-ivory sculpture of a bison.

"Thank you, Edur. I have had good reports about you. Indeed, I would be pleased to discuss this matter. I noticed your daughter's presence in the camp but did not realize who she was.

"Yet there is another matter I would like to speak of first." Ené hesitated. "A woman from our clan may have appeared in your territory some cold seasons ago. Benat, our Headman, and our trackers have always thought it was rogue hunters from the Pine Barrens who kidnapped Urtzi's wife while she was collecting hazelnuts. Do you know anything of this?"

"I wondered where a strange woman came from," Edur said slowly. "Ten cold seasons ago, she appeared in a neighbouring camp. She was treated like a slave — not well — and soon she refused to eat. She became ill and died shortly after she arrived. I was troubled by those events."

Leopard's Paw bowed his head in silence for a few moments. He lifted his head at last. "Perhaps a way can be found to make amends. A gift from friends in the Pine Barrens to the Bear Clan would be gratefully received, I am sure. Again, I welcome you both. We should talk privately. Sev and Lorea, leave us for a few moments."

Sev was torn between his numb exhaustion telling him to go back to sleep and the desire to listen to the adults' conversation. But both were overcome by the yearning to speak to Lorea. Wrapping his lynx robe tightly around himself, he shook his head to clear it. Then he stood and followed Lorea a short distance down the path.

When she turned to face him, she seemed to be hiding a smile.

"I thought you left," he began groggily.

"We did. As my father said, we were staying at the Bear cousins' camp when word came that Raven's Eye and his family stole your father's prize blade. My father decided to come back to renegotiate the marriage arrangements. Didn't you hear what he said?"

"Sorry, I missed most of it. I'm still very tired from the initiation." He showed her the three cuts on his upper arm.

"Put some fir sap and crushed fir needles on those wounds so they'll heal properly. You *do* look tired. And you look different with your hair cut off. But older, too — more dignified. I like it."

Sev felt his cheeks warm and lowered his head to hide them.

"So, what's your father talking to my father about?"

"A marriage alliance between our families. Didn't you hear that either?"

Sev blinked and rubbed the stubble on his head.

"They're talking about us getting married?"

"Yes!" Now her smile was unmistakable. "My father is determined to make an alliance with the Bears. If he and your father can agree on terms, you and I can live together in a few years! Would you like that? I know I would."

Sev's head swam.

Am I still dreaming?

"I can't believe it, I just can't — I can't believe it!" He reached for a nearby tree trunk, his legs suddenly feeling weak again "Maybe, maybe spirits *do* exist. When I was in the Cave of Lions during my initiation, I saw a pair of big yellow eyes, like a leopard's, watching me. It wasn't a real leopard — at least, not a *live* one. It could have been a spirit leopard — or maybe only a dream. But I felt protected. I thought they looked like the visionstone that you gave me. Do you think—?"

Lorea leaned forward and touched her forehead to his. They stood together silently like that for what seemed a long time.

Finally, when Sev had almost forgotten his question, she took a step back.

"I *do* think there are spirits protecting us. I don't know whether they're animal or ancestor spirits, but I think it's important to treat them properly. It certainly can't hurt. I think it helps."

Impulsively, Sev hugged her.

"My father and I are going back to the Pine Barrens now. I may not see you until next leaf-fall season. But I know my father wants the arrangement between our families to work."

"So do I."

They walked back to the fire in silence. When they reached the camp, Sev was delighted to see contentment on the two men's faces.

"Time to go," announced Edur. "I am pleased to have met you, Sun Server. We will see each other again."

He turned to Leopard's Paw. "When I return to Luku in the Pine Barrens, I will do my best to secure compensation from our Headman for Urtzi and your clan to make amends for the insult and your loss. We do not have such wealth as the Bear Clan has, but I hope our gifts will be received with good understanding. A marriage alliance between our families will bring many benefits to both of us and our kin.

"Come now, Lorea."

Lorea followed her father. When she turned to look back at Sev, she was still smiling.

Sev's father cleared his throat. "Son, I have encouraged Edur in his request for a marriage alliance between our families, but I would like to know that you agree. If his daughter is to your liking, we will exchange gifts next leaf-fall season."

Sev lowered his head to conceal his broad smile.

This feels so unreal. But my arm is still sharp with pain, so it must be real.

"Yes, Father. I agree."

"Good. It is settled, then. You must heal your wounds. And don't forget to beware of Raven's Eye. But I believe you will continue to succeed as you have done over the last Moons."

Still tired and hungry, Sev nonetheless was elated. He was a respected member of the Bear Clan now, and soon everyone would know that it was he who had killed the wolf. He had a good family and good friends in Aros and Runt, and he'd thwarted the last abuses that Bakar had hurled at him.

He still wondered whether the visions he had seen were from real spirits, but maybe there were forces involved that he didn't understand — forces that had favoured him.

But none of these things remained uppermost in his mind for long. As he settled back down by the fire, he grasped the visionstone in his palm. He thought of two amber eyes watching him, and of the touch of Lorea's forehead against his, and he kept smiling.

GLOSSARY

aurochs: a large wild bull, driven to final extinction in seventeenth-century Europe

blade: an elongated flake usually of flint; also sometimes used to refer to long bifacially flaked knives or prestige bifaces

cache: a location for storing items, especially food, typically either a pit or a small, box-like structure raised on stilts

cave leopard, cave lion: species of felines in Ice Age Europe that kept dens in caves; now extinct

Centre Star: Polaris, the pole star

cheek clicks: a sound of approval made by sucking the side of one cheek followed by a sudden release which makes a sound resembling a click

dart: a form of short spear about two metres long, meant to be thrown with a spearthrower; the end of the dart was indented and placed on a hook at the end of the spearthrower to propel the dart (see 'spearthrower')

dibat necklace: a necklace of special beads or pendants meant for show and protection

ford, fording: shallow places in a river where it is easier to cross from one bank to the opposite shore

hammerstone: a stone used for striking flakes off of flint cores

Headman: the political leader of a community who leads by recruiting supporters through gifts and debts

honour name: a name given to individuals who have achieved, and paid for, a certain rank in a community or organization

hoop drum: a circular drum held upright in one hand and beaten with a stick in the other hand; a typical shaman's drum

kurkan: dried and smoked reindeer meat, usually in long, thin strips similar to jerky

Lion Lodge: a secret society type of tribal ritual organization, typically costly to enter but powerful in community affairs

maggots: fly larvae

reindeer: cervids, closely related to North American caribou, adapted to tundra or cold forest conditions that formerly were a staple food in Upper Paleolithic Europe; today, they are the major food source for groups in the North American Arctic, Siberia and northern Scandinavia

spearthrower: a shaft of wood or antler about a metre long with a hook on its end where the end of a spear or dart is placed; it is used to propel darts (spears) with greater leverage and force than possible with spears thrown by hand (see 'dart')

starstone: white vein quartz

sunstone: clear crystal quartz

Sun's Follower: the planet Venus

thunderstone: flint

toka: a game in which one player tries to guess which hand of his opponent holds a special object (stone, shell, piece of antler). Hands are held behind the player's back and the object shuffled back and forth until the guess. Singing, betting and invoking supernatural aid are usual features of playing.

tunic: a smock kind of garment usually extending to the knees

tusk shell: dentalium shell in the form of a miniature tusk, usually about two centimetres long and found in shore waters several metres deep; used to decorate clothing, caps and bracelets in the Upper Paleolithic and traded over long distances

visionstone: amber

Xixain spirits: malevolent spirits that steal souls and cause sickness; shamans typically go into trance to battle these spirits and return the stolen soul to sick individuals

A NOTE ON THE SETTING

The setting for this story is based on a real place that is often referred to as the heartland of prehistory in France.

It is Les Eyzies-de-Tayac along the Vézère River, a river deeply incised between limestone cliffs. Many of the most famous Stone Age sites in Europe are located in the vicinity of Les Eyzies, including many of the most famous painted caves like Lascaux, Font-de-Gaume and Rouffignac. The site of Laugerie was one of several major prehistoric encampments along the Vézère, just outside Les Eyzies and right by a river fording.

However, the story does not depict any specific archaeological sites. Rather the encampment and painted cave represent general archaeological sites that were used in this area or sites that must have been destroyed or deeply buried by river movements. There are also many painted caves; my description of the Cave of the Lions is a composite view drawn from a number of real examples of caves I have visited.

Most of the details of the story are based on actual archaeological or ethnographic evidence, although the interpretations of how this all fits together are my own.

CHARACTERS AND BASQUE NAMES

Ametza ('acorn'): Urtzi's wife

Aros: a friend of Sev

Asha: the second wife of Ené

Baca: Xabi's mother

Bakar ('alone'): Sev's antagonist

Benat ('brave as a bear'): Headman of the Bears

Edur ('snow'): Lorea's father

Ekain ('summer'): hunt leader for the Bears

Ené: Sev's father

Eneko ('fiery'): Aros's older brother

Irati ('fern field'): an unmatched girl

Izar ('star'): Shaman of the Bears

Kip: one of Bakar's friends

Kiré: Sev's uncle, the brother of Ené

Leopard's Paw: the honour name for Ené

Lorea: ('flower'): a girl from the Pine Barrens

Nahia ('desire'): Ené's sister, Sev's aunt

Osane ('remedy'): Sev's sister

Perra: Osane's friend

Raven's Eye: Bakar's father

Runt: Sev's friend

Urtzi ('sky'): an old widower

Xabi: a friend of Bakar

Yana: Sev's mother

Yurok: Xabi's father

ACKNOWLEDGEMENTS

This book would not have happened without the encouragement of Suzanne Villeneuve and Mike Katz to undertake its writing, and I am very thankful to them. The fine editing and writing assistance of Mike Katz, Lisa Ferdman, Aislinn Cottell and Marianne Ward have vastly improved the original form of the story and text. Judith Cowan, Ethan Symons-Ferraro and Claire McCague provided additional helpful readings and suggestions. I was extremely fortunate to have Eric Carlson create illustrations for the story, and I would like to thank Jo Blackmore and Jessica Kaplan for their support and good help as publishers in making this story available to readers interested in life twenty thousand years ago, at least as I can best reconstruct it from archaeological remains and ethnographic comparisons to historic hunters and gatherers. As well, many thanks to Arlene Hayden for assistance in choosing type fonts and the image for the cover. And thanks to Omar Gallegos for an eye-pleasing design that captures the intention of the book.

Dr. Brian Hayden is an author and archaeologist who has conducted research on four continents. His passion is to understand what cultures were like in the past — especially hunting and gathering cultures — and why they have changed. He obtained a Certificate of Prehistory at the University of Bordeaux, and he studied stone-tool making with Australian Aborigines. His doctoral degree is in archaeology from the University of Toronto. For thirty years, he worked with Indigenous groups in the interior of British Columbia, recording their traditional uses of food resources and excavating an amazing prehistoric winter village at Keatley Creek.

Now a Professor Emeritus of Archaeology at Simon Fraser University and Honorary Research Associate of the Anthropology Department at the University of British Columbia, Dr. Brian Hayden has published numerous professional journal articles and books, including works on the Old Stone Age in France and a landmark synthesis of prehistoric religion. His research has been recognized by his induction into the Royal Society of Canada. Originally born in New York, Dr. Hayden now lives on Cortes Island, in coastal British Columbia.

Some of his most notable work includes:

- *Shamans, Sorcerers, and Saints: The Prehistory of Religion* (Smithsonian Publications, 2003)

- *The Power of Feasts* (Cambridge University Press, 2014)

- *The Power of Ritual in Prehistory: Secret Societies and the Origins of Social Complexity* (Cambridge University Press, 2018)

To learn more, please see:
brianhaydenauthor.com
www.sfu.ca/archaeology-old/dept/fac_bio/hayden/